WITCH'S BLOCK

THE ACCIDENTAL MEDIUM BOOK ONE

AMY BOYLES

LADYBUGBOOKS LLC

At forty-three, Paige Provey is at the height of her career. As the author of a successful paranormal book series, she has a legion of fans who all believe she has powers herself. But when Paige's ex-husband reveals that she's a fraud, she quickly finds herself and her career canceled.

But Paige is still under a publishing contract, so she must put out a new book--one that will save her career. The only problem is her crippling case of writer's block. So she heads to a lakeside community to refill her creative well.

Only while she's there strange things begin to happen: Paige speaks to a woman who she swears is transparent, and everyone in town dresses as if it's Halloween. Not only that, but there's a very mysterious (and attractive) man who claims to hunt monsters.

As if that's not weird enough, when Paige's ex-husband winds up dead, she becomes the primary suspect in his murder. Can Paige write another book, figure out the mystery surrounding Willow Lake, and also prove her innocence? Or will all her dreams go up in flames?

CHAPTER 1

I see ghosts.
        Sort of.
    Not really.

Okay, I don't see ghosts. I've never seen one ghost.

But up until six months ago, the entire continent of North America believed very differently.

"Ms. Provey, are you ready? You're on in one minute."

"Thanks," I told the production assistant from the wings of the stage. She shivered as a the air-conditioning unit above us turned on.

"Cold?" I whispered.

"Always. I forgot my sweater."

I slipped out of my Versace cardigan. "Here, take this. You can't stand back here all day freezing."

"No, I can't." She spotted the label and her eyes widened. The assistant pushed it back into my hands. "I can't wear this."

"I insist, and I won't hear another word of argument."

She hesitated before beaming. "I'll get it back to you."

I shrugged. "No big deal if you don't. You have a long day ahead. Stay warm."

Out front, several hundred people were gathered to spend the morning with Dakota Flynn, the biggest name in daytime television.

Dakota, dressed in white silk, sat on a plush cream-colored chair beside a chocolate-brown sofa—the place where I was supposed to settle my rear end in less than one minute.

"Our next guest," Dakota said into the cameras, "is a New York Times best-selling author of ghost mysteries. She even has one living in her house, and he's supposedly the muse for her very successful *Ghost Out* series. Please welcome Paige Provey."

"And go," the production assistant said.

I tossed my brown hair back and headed out with a smile, my straight teeth more than likely gleaming from the recent whitening I'd had done on them.

"So good to see you," Dakota said, sweeping me into a friendly hug. "Please, have a seat."

Folks kept clapping, so I waved to the audience.

"Everyone settle down," Dakota teased. "Let's let Paige speak; then you can clap again."

"I love you, Paige," someone shouted.

"Thank you," I said demurely.

When the applause died, Dakota turned to me. "So Paige, you are such a phenomenon. People love your books. They love *you*. You have given a voice to those who have witnessed the other side, the paranormal veil of life, but were afraid to speak out. We all want to know how you do it. But first"—she held up my newest release—"before I forget, everyone at home, be sure to grab Paige's latest release, *Ghost of a Chance*, and for those of you in the audience, check under your seats because each of you have a copy." The audience squealed with delight. When they calmed, Dakota motioned to me. "Tell us everything, Paige —have you always seen spirits?"

"Well, um, I never really saw much when I was a kid, but it was when I moved into my house that Thomas appeared." The audience clapped. Thomas was always a popular subject. "He is a ghost, and at first he would just move things around the house, but then he started talking and telling me things. That's how I first came up with the series idea for *Ghost Out.* I felt that people needed to know Thomas's story."

Yes, it was all a load of crap. There was no Thomas. But loads of crap sold books, and I was riding my gravy train for as long as I possibly could.

Also I was going through a messy divorce and desperately needed all the extra money that I could get my hands on because my soon-to-be ex was taking me to the cleaners.

"Well, you have really touched so many folks with your humor and sympathy for the spirit world," Dakota said. "You are just such a national treasure. I know that *I* treasure you." She turned to the audience. "Who else treasures Paige with her Southern wit and gothic tales of ghosts?"

The audience erupted in applause. Honestly it was a tad bit embarrassing. But great for book sales.

"Okay," Dakota said, rising. "It's time to take some questions from the audience. If anyone has a question for Paige, raise your hand."

Dakota sprinted into the audience with the energy of a bobcat.

A woman in a red sweater a few rows in raised her hand.

Dakota held the microphone to her chin. "What's your question?"

The woman's face turned bright red from nervousness. "I just want to know, Ms. Provey, how do you come up with your ideas? You're on book ten of the series. How do you keep having new things to write about?"

"Well, honestly, it's Thomas. He just keeps whispering in my ear. He's got stories to tell, so I type them on my computer. I have him to thank for all my success."

"Okay, next question." Dakota headed over to a young woman in glasses in the very back. "What would you like to ask Ms. Provey?"

"I just want to say," the woman replied, voice shaking, "that your books have completely touched my life. They changed me. You have inspired me so much that before, I wasn't heeding my calling, but because of you and your courage to tell Thomas's tale, I have the will to follow my own dreams. That's all I had to say."

She blew kisses to me as I spoke. "Thank you so much. I am so blessed to have amazing readers like you in my life."

"We have time for one more," Dakota said. "Yes, you in the front."

She stopped in front of a young woman with long dark hair sitting smack in the front row. "What's your question?"

The woman cleared her throat.

"Don't be nervous," I said. "We're all friends here."

The woman pushed a pair of glasses up her nose. "I wanted to know what it feels like to be a fraud."

My heart stuttered. "I'm sorry?"

The woman's voice loudened. "You've been lying to these people, telling them that you speak to ghosts and taking their money, when in reality you've never spoken to one spirit ever."

"That's not true," I replied, clutching my hands nervously.

She pulled out her phone and up came a video. "That's not what your ex-husband said."

Then, loud as dynamite exploding, came Walter's voice through the speaker on her phone. *"Paige? Paige's never seen a ghost in her entire life. She makes it all up, letting folks believe in her. She's full of crap."*

Dakota's jaw dropped. She slowly pivoted toward me. "Well, Paige, what do you have to say to that?"

My heart raced. My mouth became a desert. Finally, words came. "Walter, we're going through a divorce. He's only saying that to get me to support him financially." I laughed nervously. "If he tells lies about me and I go begging him to stop it, he'll recant what he said."

The woman sneered. "Really? There's more."

She pressed the video again. Walter's voice pierced the silence in the studio. *"Paige wants me to stop talking, but I've always loved her. She's trying to ruin me and take everything I brought into this marriage. That's why I want the world to know the truth about her."*

Then the jerk broke into tears. This looked bad for me. Very, very bad.

I was about to speak, to say something to save my skin, when the young woman beat me to it.

"Paige Provey, looks like you've been canceled."

CHAPTER 2

"This will blow over," Madeleine, my agent, said right after it all happened.

"I don't know," I replied, lying in bed with the covers up to my chin, my phone in hand as I checked my Twitter feed. "It's everywhere. The video of Walter and the clip from the Dakota show. I'm ruined."

"Not necessarily." Madeleine bit into something; it sounded like an apple. She spoke between chewing. "The publisher hasn't canceled your contract yet. When they call, I'll talk to them about putting you under a pen name or holding your next book until this dies down, because it will, Paige. Don't worry."

Well, it was now six months later and the story had not died. In fact, my book sales had hit an all-time low. Walter had taken just about everything in the divorce, and my only hope was to rejuvenate myself in the healing waters of Willow Lake.

"So you're staying here for the summer, is it?"

I followed the cabin owner, Mrs. Patricia Beaker, into the small rental.

It looked nothing like the pictures. On the website the cottage had window boxes filled with flowers and pretty green curtains. Oh, it still had the boxes, but they were full of weeds, and the curtains were frayed, the fabric rotten to the point that it looked ready to fall off the bar it hung from.

The scent of must wafted up my nose. Patricia turned around and smiled weakly. "Place needs to be aired out. I'll just open a window."

She did so and turned back, caught a glimpse of my one suitcase. "Is that all the luggage you have? Won't you need more for the summer? I figure an author like yourself would have lots of stuff—you know, you'd bring books and all that."

I smiled. "I have them all on an e-reader."

"Oh, one of them Kindle things."

"Right." I set the suitcase down and stared out the window. "Wow. That's quite a view."

Patricia placed her hands on her hips. "That's what folks come to Willow Lake for—to relax and rejuvenate."

The view was incredible. Tall pines bracketed the lake, revealing an S-shaped body of water that disappeared into the horizon. It was early in the morning, and the only person on the crystal waters was a lone fisherman.

Patricia cocked a brow at me. "What kind of books is it you write again? I got a nephew who loves to read. When I told him a famous author was coming to stay, he demanded I find out what you'd written." She chuckled. "He about pinned one arm behind my back wanting an autograph, but I told him that we'd get to that."

I smiled. "Oh, I write books with ghosts in them."

She smirked. "Folks like that kind of stuff?"

"Surprisingly they do."

The landlady pulled the ball cap from her head and scratched at the gray curls beneath. "Do you believe in all that supernatural stuff? I ain't never seen a ghost, but I wouldn't be surprised if a house or two in town was haunted."

"Me? No, I don't believe in spirits or witches. All of it's made-up. It's just fun to write about, is all."

She shot me a peculiar look before saying, "Let me show you around the rest of the house." She pointed to a wall lined with cabinets. "That's the kitchen. Through that door's the bedroom." She pointed to the right. "And through that one's the bathroom. To get the air conditioner to work right, don't put it any lower than sixty-eight degrees. If you put it on sixty-seven, it'll freeze up and I'll have to call the repairman to come out. So, sixty-eight. That's the lowest she'll go. I'd tell you the trick to working the heat, but you won't be here past September."

"Right."

"Three months, that's all you're staying."

"It gives me the time I need to write my novel."

Patricia jabbed the air with her finger. "That reminds me—I brought you a desk, just like you requested. Let me get it out of the truck."

"I'll come, too."

I followed her out, and she opened the hatchback of her SUV. "Here it is. It ain't nothing fancy, but it'll do, I reckon."

The gray desk was small and slender and just wide enough to house my computer and an entire pot of coffee. "It's perfect."

I helped her bring it inside, and we pushed it back against the wall. When we were finished, Patricia eyed our work with pride, as if we'd just spent all day sawing and hammering the desk into creation.

"So you gonna write about them ghosts here in this house?"

Well, if I came up with an idea, I would. Ever since the big Dakota Flynn debacle, I'd hit a huge patch of writer's block, which was a problem as I was still under contract.

And that reminded me—there was an email on my computer from my agent that I had to reply to. I'd been putting it off and off. My next book was due in three months, and she had yet to see hide nor hair of it.

Well, that would be because I hadn't written a single line yet.

Patricia placed her meaty hands on her hips. "So you think this house'll give you ideas?"

"I hope so," I said with a sigh. "If the view is any hint, then I'll be writing up a storm."

She slapped her hands. "That reminds me. There are some books and games here, in the bedroom."

I followed her into the tiny room and discovered a built-in bookcase lining the small wall that the door was on. "If you get tired of reading books on your Kindle or whatever you use, there are some old-fashioned ones here."

"Thank you," I told her.

"The owner before me loved to read, and when she passed away, I never got to taking the books out. Seemed like I'd be spitting on the dead; you know what I mean?"

"Sure do," I said, not at all sure that I agreed.

"Well, I'll be going then." She headed toward the front door. "I just need that check from you."

"Oh, right. All three months in advance; that's what we agreed on." My stomach tightened even as I said it. Patricia had wanted to be paid up front, which was sort of a problem as I was nearly broke.

Wished I was joking.

I pulled the prewritten check from my purse and handed it over. Patricia inspected it like she was scouring the bottom of the sea for treasure.

"Paige Provey, what a name. I like the way it sounds. Bet you got lots of folks who like the way it sounds, too."

"Umm," I said, unsure of what she meant.

"Folks come out of the woodwork because of your rich-sounding name," she elaborated.

"Oh, well, if you count ex-husbands who demand alimony, but who are also so stupid that they ruin your career, then yes, I suppose I've got one of those."

Patricia's eyes twinkled with interest. "That sounds like a humdinger of a situation. Hope that means your check won't bounce." She snapped the paper for emphasis. "'Sides, you got a lot of fancy stuff. He couldn't be taking you for that much money."

There, Patricia would have been wrong. My ex wanted every cent I made, and then some. "Well, he doesn't work."

"Disabled?" she asked, shaking her head.

"Yes, fell out of a tree."

"That's terrible. What took him up there?"

"Our next-door neighbor was undressing," I told her.

Patricia's jaw dropped. "Come again?"

"My ex is a real piece of work." I sighed and ran my fingers through my brown hair that was threaded here and there with silvery grays. "We had a hot little number for a next-door neighbor, and so he climbed into a tree to watch her undress like a teenage boy. That's how he fell. I divorced him but got stuck paying alimony because he broke his back."

Patricia opened her mouth and then shut it. Guess I'd taken the words right out of her mouth with that story.

She cleared her throat and managed, "You need anything, you just holler. If you need me to, I'll send my nephew to make sure that you're settling in okay."

I waved away her concern. "That won't be necessary."

"If you're hungry, there's a great grill in town named Only Steak. They serve a mean buffet breakfast, too, lots of grits and down-home cooking." She opened the front door and tapped the frame. "Just call if you need something."

"Will do. Thank you."

"See you."

With that, Patricia shut the door and I was left alone—all alone to write.

I set about putting my clothes away and placing my computer on the table. I made some instant coffee that I'd brought and sat at the desk, staring out the window hoping for an idea. Any idea.

Thirty minutes in and I still hadn't written one word. The sun was high and the water sparkling.

I inhaled, exhaled and finally lifted the top of my computer. After opening a new file, I settled back and waited for the muse to strike.

It did not.

"All right. Get up. Find something to do."

I rose and paced the room, doing my best to spit out ideas. Deciding that I was done with ghosts, I thought about giving witches a try. "A witch who can see into the past but who can't see her own future. No, that's been done. A witch with a terrible memory suddenly remembers everything. Ugh. Those are horrible."

With nothing coming to mind, I headed into the bedroom to take a look at the bookshelves. "Tolstoy, Laura Ingalls Wilder, C.S. Lewis. Wow, what a collection."

My phone dinged and I pulled it from my pocket. Walter's name lit up the screen. *I haven't gotten your monthly payment yet.*

"Argh!" I threw the phone on the bed. "I don't want to pay you, you jerk!"

It was because of Walter that I was broke. His actions had gotten me canceled. On top of that, a judge had ruled that I owed Walter alimony since he couldn't work anymore because of his broken back.

No, the judge hadn't believed the story that my husband was spying on our neighbor.

I'd sold the house to pay for the divorce, and now all I had were a few thousand dollars in my bank account. If I only ate ramen noodles, I could survive until my next book sold.

But I was plumb out of ideas.

I dropped onto the bed in frustration and stared at the bookshelves. There, poking out of from the black and brown spines, sat a purple-covered book.

That was curious.

The book sat on the top of the shelf, which was about three feet taller than me. From that distance I couldn't read the title, so I grabbed a chair from the kitchen and stood on it.

"*A Study in The Paranormal* by Heronomous Spell." I couldn't help but scoff. What a horrible title and what an obvious pen name. But that didn't stop me from sliding the book from the shelf. "What are you about?"

The spine cracked when I peeled back the cover. Inside I found a mix of stories. There were ghost stories and monster tales, all sorts of things.

"The Tale of the Woman Trapped in a Book," was the very first story. It was a quick read and told about a woman who'd found a magic book and became so entranced by it that she got sucked into it, never to be seen again.

There was even a picture to go with it—a woman in plain clothes doing the laundry.

"Not sure what laundry has to do with magic, but whatever." I chuckled and slipped the book back onto the shelf. "Well, that was fun." But it didn't inspire me.

I stepped down from the chair and pushed it away, but my aim was off. The chair bumped into the case and the books shuddered.

I glanced up in time to see the purple book fall off the shelf, aiming straight for my head.

Next thing I knew, everything had gone black.

CHAPTER 3

"*H*ey, you all right? You hit yourself pretty hard on the head."

I slowly opened my eyes. "Ugh. That book. It fell." My head pounded. I tentatively touched the spot of impact. It was tender, throbbing. "Ouch. Who would have thought a simple book would hurt so much?"

"That old book is full of mischief. But now, sweetie, are you okay?"

I blinked at the woman standing in front of me. She had platinum hair and big green eyes that peered curiously at me.

"Wait. Who are you? How'd you get in here?"

"Me? Oh, I was trapped in that book. You let me out when you dropped it."

I laughed. "Ha, ha. Very funny." I pushed myself up and studied her. "Did Patricia send you over?"

"Who's Patricia? Sweetie, I don't know any Patricias."

She was very pretty, with dimples on both cheeks. It was while I stared at her that I noticed something quite funny about the woman. Her clothes were very thin. I could almost see through them.

I peered closer and realized that I *could* see through them. In fact, she was transparent, too.

I gasped. "I can see through you!"

She gasped. "You can? Oh no, I must be a ghost!"

I closed my eyes. "None of this is real. You aren't real."

"But I sound so real."

"Okay, you're real. But I can't see through you. You are as solid as a tree. You are as solid as a tree. I know that I sound insane right now. Please just go with it. I promise that I'm not normally so scatterbrained. Don't tell Patricia."

Oh, what did it matter if Patricia knew? She had my check already, just about all the money that I had in the entire world. If she thought I was crazy, it shouldn't matter because I had paid up.

"I don't know any Patricias," the woman said again. "I told you that I fell out of that book."

On that, I opened my eyes. It had been long enough for them to right themselves, I figured. The woman would now be solid as stone. I swept my gaze toward her and smiled.

But she was still see-through.

I could clearly make out the bed, the walls, even the window through her.

"Look"—I scrambled to my feet—"just lock up when you're done. I'm going out for a breath of fresh air. And some food. I really need food. My blood sugar is low. Can't even remember the last time that I ate. I'll be back."

I darted from the room, grabbing my purse and computer on the way out the door. As soon as I was inside my car, I inhaled and exhaled deeply.

"She said that she was going to send her nephew. Why would she send her niece?" I jammed my keys into the ignition and started up the engine. "And why wouldn't that woman just admit that she knew Patricia? Ugh. I'm going to hate it here in Willow Lake. I can already tell."

But that didn't matter, I thought as I pointed my car toward town. I was only going to be here for a few months. Just long enough to write my next book. If I ever got any inspiration for it.

The main strip of downtown was robust, housing several clothing boutiques, a hardware store, a burger place, and a breakfast joint. The grill Patricia had mentioned was just at the end of the block. I parked and exhaled again.

"Food. I need food."

I went inside and didn't bother to be seated. I headed straight to the bar. For early afternoon, the place was busy. Lots of parents dragging around kids with wet hair. They'd probably come straight off the lake for a late lunch.

I tapped my fingers on the counter, waiting for the bartender to appear. After a minute a small older man popped up from behind the counter.

"What can I do for you, lass?"

He was Irish and living in the South. How interesting. "I'd like a Jack and Coke, please."

"Oh, it's been one of those days, has it?"

I rolled my eyes. I didn't need to spill my guts to an old bartender. Not unless he could help me write a book. He fixed the drink and placed it in front of me.

"Will you be eating?"

"Yes, please."

He pulled a menu out from under the counter and slapped it on the bar top. "There you are. They make a mean french onion soup in the back."

My stomach rumbled. "Sounds good."

He waved his hand. "The best."

"I'll take it with a side of onion rings."

"Oh, those are to die for, too."

I couldn't help but smile at his exuberance. "Good. I can't wait to try them."

He walked away to place the order, and I sipped the drink. As the liquid slid into my stomach, I immediately started to feel my nerves calm. Thank goodness. I didn't know why I'd thought that woman was transparent. Had I lost my mind?

Stress. It was all stress.

"What brings you here?" the bartender asked.

"I'm staying for the summer."

"Oh, you here to experience the healing waters of Willow Lake?"

"Something like that."

He polished a glass as he spoke. "Name's Ferguson. But you can call me Fergie if you want."

"Only if you break out into song," I joked.

He got that I was talking about the female singer and hooted with laughter. "That's a good one." Fergie cocked a brow at me. "You ever been here before?"

"Yes, I have. My ex-husband and I used to come up here when we first married."

"It's beautiful, it is."

The bar door opened, slamming into the wall with a *boom*. Every person in the restaurant turned around to see who or what had caused the noise. There in the doorway stood a tall man with shoulder-length hair and a beard. He carried a knapsack and looked as if he'd just come in from hitchhiking off the interstate.

"Fergie," the man said, his smile wide.

"Grim," Ferguson called out. "Come and have a drink."

Grim was a lumberjack of a man, probably close to thirty-five, seven or eight years behind my forty-three. Shh. Don't tell anyone I told you.

He dropped onto a seat two barstools away, bringing with him the scent of spice—dark, deep, heady. He tossed his knapsack on the counter. "I'd love a beer. Been a while since I had one."

Where had he been, the Arctic Circle?

"Coming right up."

Fergie whistled as he poured the beer, which had a frothy head when the bartender slapped it down in front of Grim. Not that I was watching, of course.

"Everything go good?" Fergie asked.

"As well as it could have," Grim replied, his tone almost like a hum.

It was impossible not to watch this larger-than-life man. Grim was all wilderness, and yet he seemed to have a sophistication that I didn't expect.

Not that I was staring or anything, but his fingernails were trimmed, neat, clean of any dirt, and his clothing, though it was rustic, wasn't dingy or even rumpled. He was well put together.

"Soup's up." Fergie placed my bowl of steaming soup and the onion rings in front of me. "Enjoy."

I was about to dig in when a *thunk* caught my attention. I glanced to my left, by Grim, and noticed the knapsack was intruding on my space.

Just a second ago it had been closer to him. At least I thought it had been. I still must've been suffering from residual low blood sugar.

I dug into my soup. The cheese-topped bread broke away easily, allowing me to grab a big spoonful of broth and bready goodness. The liquid spilled over my tongue, sending an array of flavors washing down my throat.

I moaned. "Oh wow. This is amazing."

The onion rings were also perfection, fried to a beautiful golden brown. They crunched when I bit into them. This was heaven.

I closed my eyes for a moment, and when I opened them, the knapsack was right beside my wrist.

I turned to Grim. "Sorry, but it looks like your bag seems to have made its way over here."

I'd said it as a joke, but Grim's face darkened. "You must be mistaken."

Um. No, I wasn't. "Well, okay. But when you sat down, it was beside you, and now it's beside me. So either you pushed it, or it walked over."

Grim and Fergie exchanged a look that I couldn't read. "I must've moved it with my hand." Grim pulled the sack back toward himself.

There. That was done. Though part of me wished that the big, hulking, beautiful man would have talked to me more, I went back to my soup.

Until the knapsack hit my arm again. It was impossible to keep the annoyance from my voice. "Your bag. Again. It's on top of me."

At that point it was. The knapsack had been pushed so far that it was slowly creeping over my arm.

"Sorry, but your bag," I said forcefully.

What was it with this guy? He might've been pretty to look at, but he had no clue when it came to personal space. Like, none.

Grim shot me a hard look. "It's not even beside you."

I looked back down again and it wasn't. The bag was beside Grim. Had I been imagining it? Was I completely cracking up?

"Grim," Fergie said, "this is our newest resident..." He cocked his brows, waiting for me to fill in my name.

"Paige Provey," I said. "I'm here for the summer."

Grim nodded like he could have cared less. "Well, if you're going to stay here, I suggest that you have your eyes checked so that you don't casually accuse people of doing things that they aren't."

My cheeks burned flaming hot. I was not going to be put down by this guy. "Look, your bag was there, beside me."

"Ma'am, bags don't get up and crawl on their own."

"Yours did," I said coldly.

He smiled, and if I hadn't disliked him so much in that moment, I might've melted from it. But never in my life had I so instantly met someone that I disliked. Really. Honestly. Never. Like, never never.

Who tells someone when they first meet that they need glasses? I already wore bifocals. Progressive lenses, to be exact. But I wasn't about to admit to Mr. Thirtysomething that I was so old that I had to wear his grandmother's lenses.

I lifted my chin. "I'm sorry. I wasn't trying to be difficult; it was just that I know what I saw. I apologize that your big muscular arm has a problem staying in its own space. Perhaps I'm not the one who needs glasses."

And feeling very smug, I turned back to my food and began eating again.

Only, the bag made its way over once more. This time I swore that I saw the imprint of a nose sniffing at my soup.

I jumped off the barstool and pointed at it. "It moved. The bag! It moved. You've got a creature in there. Is that even legal? You can't bring animals into a restaurant; you'll give everyone hepatitis!"

Okay, probably not even close to being accurate, but I just went with it.

Grim pulled his knapsack back over and rose. He shot me a dark look and then said to Ferguson, "Looks like I'll be going."

He started to head out when the door banged open again. What was it with this place?

There, standing in the doorway, was a face I knew all too well.

My ex-husband, Weasel—I mean *Walter*—sneered at me. "There you are, Paige. I knew I'd find you. I want my money—every last dime that you owe me."

Oh crap. This day was going from bad to worse.

CHAPTER 4

"Walter, what are you doing here?" Ruining my soup and my onion rings, I nearly added. Couldn't a gal grab a bite to eat without a man shoving a knapsack at her and without her peeping Tom of an ex-husband showing up?

Where was the justice?

"I want my money," he said, sticking his finger in my nose. "And I want it now."

All right. I had two choices. I could stand in the middle of a restaurant and be completely embarrassed in front of the really hot but annoying Grim, or I could grab Walter and go outside to talk about it.

Not wanting to give my new friend the lumberjack any reason to laugh in my face, I motioned for Walter to follow me outside.

Once we were in the open, he started again. "Where's my money, Paige?"

Up your butt with a coconut, I nearly bit back. "How did you find me?"

Walter laced his fingers together and placed them atop his balding head. "What? You think I couldn't figure out that you'd come here after you sold my house? You loved this place."

"For your information, I sold the house to pay for my lawyer and to support your lifestyle."

He scoffed. "What lifestyle is that?"

"Sitting on the couch eating Cheetos while waiting for your neighbor to undress."

Walter blanched. "I never did that. I told you."

"All evidence points to yes. Listen, I paid you last month's check."

"I need this month's," he demanded, spit flying from his mouth. "You're behind."

He wasn't lying. I was behind. The truth was, I was hoping to put Walter off for a couple of months while I wrote the book. When I got my advance, then I'd pay him. But of course I didn't want to tell him that.

"You still can't write, can you," he said snidely. "I hope your creative well isn't drying up, because that would be bad for you."

People were going in and out of the restaurant, watching us curiously. I smiled, hoping we just looked like a couple of folks chatting, but I knew we looked like a bickering couple.

"For your information, my well isn't dry. I've had a fantastic idea for a new series."

"Then give me my money. What's stopping you? I want that money by tomorrow or else."

Paying him tomorrow would take every last dime that I had. It would make me one step away from being homeless, from becoming a madwoman who talked to myself.

I could just see it. In three months I'd be living on the street, under a cardboard box. I wouldn't even be living inside of it. I'd be *under* it, murmuring to myself.

Would you like some tea? I would ask myself in a British accent.

Yes, I would love some, I would reply, also in British.

The future of my life flashed before my eyes as Walter stood sneering at me, his little pig face twisted in triumph.

It was funny; when I was deeply in love with Walter ten years prior, I didn't recall ever having thought of his face as swinish. But now all I could do was focus on how his upturned nose reminded me of a pig and how his jowls really looked like they needed to be stuffed with apples and truffles.

I didn't even care if you mixed the two or not.

"I will get that money, Paige," Walter shouted into the parking lot, so that everyone, including the horrible Grim, who was also out here now, could see and hear my sweet, sweet humiliation.

I had been in this town for approximately three hours, and I already had to wear a bag on my head in order to walk down the street.

Walter had already taken my home. He had taken my marriage (which I was honestly glad to be out of since he had the whole peeping Tom quality and all), and he was helping to slowly drain my creativity because of the stress of having to deal with him.

So given all of that, it was totally understandable that the next words to leap from my mouth were—

"What is it with this day? I get hit on the head by a book, and the next thing I know, I'm having a conversation with a woman who's transparent. God, can this day get any worse?"

"I want my money," he shouted.

Right. I still had to deal with this. I jabbed my finger at him. "If you attempt to take one penny from me, then I swear to God, I'll kill you, Walter."

The words flew from my mouth before I had a chance to stop them. They just hung in the air for the entire world to witness. Someone walking through the parking lot even gasped.

Walter chuckled, amused. "You, kill someone? You can't even kill a spider, Paige. You're too afraid that it'll leap up and kill you first."

Unfortunately that was true. It was impossible for me to squash arachnids. They were just so hairy, and all those legs were terrifying. I know, I know. I shouldn't have been afraid of the small ones, but they freaked me out, too. All the eyes and legs—it gave me the shudders just thinking about it.

But Walter couldn't let my words die. He threw back his head and laughed. "The great Paige Provey wants to kill me. What are you going to do? Start telling everyone that you're a witch now? Lie to your new fans just like you did to your old ones? You going to spell me to death? You don't even see ghosts. Or have you forgotten that you lied to the American public?"

Rage like lava burned through my veins. How dare my horrible ex-husband show up, demand money and then, to get his money, drudge up the past.

"You wouldn't have to be haggling me for money," I spat, "if you hadn't told the entire world my secret. There would be plenty of it. *For me.* For you there'd be none because I would've countersued you to get every cent that you stole from me."

Walter threw back his head and laughed. "Countersued? That's rich. Who supported you when no one was buying your books? When no one wanted to read a Paige Provey novel?"

"You mean when I worked for a living waiting tables? Is that what you mean?"

"You didn't even get a job using your college degree," he said snidely, eyes glittering with triumph.

I slapped my thighs. "Do you know what an English degree allows you to be when you graduate? A bag lady, nothing more. Or maybe an administrative assistant. It is the most useless degree in the world. And I have it. You're right. Now if you would please leave me alone, I would appreciate it because I have a meal to get back to."

I was done with this conversation. Done. Walter had humiliated me, and I'd only just arrived in Willow Lake.

I turned to walk back inside, smiling at the folks who were milling about, pretending not to watch me having a knock-down, drag-out fight with my ex.

"Not so fast, Paige," Walter said.

I tightened my jaw, ticked. I stopped but did not give him the satisfaction of turning around. "What is it?"

"If you don't pay up, I'll go to the papers and tell them that you're scamming me out of money."

Oh, that was it. I did actually turn to face him. "What are you going to do? Ruin me more? Is that even possible? You've already taken my livelihood. I have to write under a pen name just so that I can publish, some name that nobody knows. I'm a writer who has no idea what to write. Now. Are we done here?"

"Oh, there you are."

I glanced to my right and saw the woman Patricia had sent over to my house for some reason. I still didn't have all those details, and at the moment I didn't actually care.

I shook my head in annoyance. Could today get any more frustrating? But instead of taking my frustration out on this poor woman who was only doing her job, I smiled.

"Is there something that I can help you with?"

She tugged at her blonde hair. "Um. No. I was just looking for you."

Why was she looking for me?

"Who are you talking to?" Walter asked.

I scoffed and jerked my hand toward the woman. "Her. She was in the cottage earlier. She must need something, so unlike you, Walter, I'm trying to be nice to people. Instead of peeping on them while they undress, I'm attempting to say hello and be friendly without spying on them while they're indecent."

"I told you that wasn't what I was doing," he shouted.

"Yes. You. Were!"

The woman turned to go. "Maybe I'll just come back later."

"No, no. You can stay." I shot Walter a withering look. "I'm done here."

"Who on earth are you talking to?" Walter demanded again.

I walked right over to the woman and pointed. "Her. I'm talking to her. She's standing right in front of you. Are you blind?"

"There's no one there!"

I stopped and scoffed. "Right. There's no one there. She's standing in front of me. She's right here. See?" I moved to grab her wrist, and my hand washed through her. I blinked. Stopped. Stared. "Um. What just happened?" I asked her.

"You can't touch me because I'm dead."

A maniac laugh bubbled from the back of my throat. "Right. You're dead. I touched you and couldn't get ahold of you because you're dead."

"Paige, you need to see a doctor," Walter said. "You can't be in charge of your own finances, not with your mental capacities like they are."

Oh. He made me so mad. I whirled on him. "My mental capacities are just fine. And you'd love that, wouldn't you? Getting your grubby little hands on my estate—or what's left of it. Walter, you need to leave. I don't ever want to see you around again."

I didn't know what was going on, why that woman was lying and saying that she was dead, or why my hand had slipped through her arm. No, I wasn't going to think about it. It didn't make sense. Ghosts didn't exist. Because I was pretty certain if they did, then they'd be lining up to haunt me since I'd made a small fortune writing about them and then getting canceled for lying about my relationship with one.

I marched toward the front of the restaurant, and that was when Walter shouted out, "I want my money, Paige."

There were maybe a dozen people outside by that time and I was through being humiliated by my ex. I whirled around and jabbed my finger. "If you ruin me, I'll get even, Walter. I won't lie down and die. You'll see. You'll regret it."

Before he could utter one more word, I stormed into the restaurant to finish my very cold meal.

CHAPTER 5

*M*y meal was indeed, frigid by the time I returned, but I finished it anyway, thanking Ferguson for the suggestion and tipping him well.

Hey, I might not have much money, but I believed in tipping. Luckily with that awful Grim gone, I was able to enjoy my chilly dinner without his knapsack attacking me.

What was up with this town, anyway? First the strange woman, and then the wandering knapsack.

Perhaps Willow Lake hadn't been the best location for me to retreat to after all.

But anyway, I returned to the cabin, and there was no sign of that woman. I made myself a cup of instant coffee, making a mental note that I needed to hit the grocery store the next morning. Otherwise my entire diet would subsist of coffee, coffee and more coffee.

Not that I was complaining.

I'd just settled down into the recliner, staring out at the lake as the sun faded into the horizon, when a head popped through the wall.

"Ah!" I jumped up, splashing coffee everywhere. "Dang it! I just washed this robe."

Then my gaze landed on the figure of that same woman as she literally slid through the outer wall and into the living room.

I picked up the closest weapon that I could find, which was an iron from the fireplace tools set on the hearth. "Who are you?" I demanded. "Why do you keep following me? And *what* are you? I swear if you come any closer, I'll run you through with this poker."

She reared back and then stopped, realizing something. "You can't run me through because like I told you, I'm already dead. I can't be killed twice unless you happen to know something that I don't."

"You're not dead. You can't be dead. That would make you a..."

And there I paused and looked, really *looked* at her. Her blonde hair was cut short, in a bob to her chin, and she wore loose-fitting yet nicely tailored clothing—capri pants and a button-down shirt. She looked familiar.

"You're the picture of the woman in that book—the woman who went missing. Oh my gosh. This cannot be happening. I've finally cracked. I've lost my mind. This is it." I stared up at the ceiling. "God, if you want to strike me with lightning and just go ahead and finish me off, do it. My entire life has gone up in smoke anyway. It's all a wash. I've no money, so I actually can't afford to go out to eat much more. I'm living in a cabin on a lake and have no idea where I'm going from here. I've got a book due in three months, and if it's not great, my publisher will drop me. It's my redemption book. I've got to make up for being canceled. And on top of all of that, I'm standing here staring at a woman who looks to have jumped out of a book."

She inspected her fingernails. "Are you finished throwing a pity party for yourself?"

"What? You can't just walk in here and tell me that I've been throwing a pity party."

She shrugged. "Look, all I know is that one minute I was in that book, and the next I'm out of it, thanks to you and your witch abilities. Of course now I'm a ghost; I'm dead. But I have you to thank. So thank you. Shall we get started?"

What was going on?

"Started? On what? What could I possibly be getting started with you except a phone call to the insane asylum so that they can lock me up and throw away the key?"

The woman sighed and sat on the couch. She sat. Like, actually sat.

"I can tell you what happened, and then you, with your witch powers, can help me."

"I am not a witch."

Her gaze started at my head, washed down to my feet and then back up to my head. "Okay, whatever you say. Look. My name's Snow Murry, and I was murdered. At least I think that I was. I mean, if you're put in the book, you're pretty much murdered. That's how it goes."

"What are you talking about?"

"The book." She widened her eyes as if I was the one who had lost my mind. Which I had. "If you end up in it, you die. That's how it is. That's what I was told, anyway."

I didn't know how to answer. "What do you mean, you die?"

She sighed and stared up at the ceiling. I imagined she was silently asking herself how in the world I couldn't keep up with the conversation. Like, what was wrong with me?

"You *die*, die. You're a witch; you should know all of this," she chastised.

"Look, I'm not a witch. I don't see ghosts. The last time I even said that I saw ghosts, I got canceled."

"What does that mean? How can a person be canceled? A TV show can, but not a person."

"Darling, what year are you from?" I joked. "In this day and age, everyone can be canceled."

"I'm from 1997."

The poker fell from my hand and clattered onto the wooden floor. "Um, well, Barney the Dinosaur could be canceled soon, too. And with that, I will gladly say good night. I'm really not in the mood to have to tell a—whatever you are—the ways and means of life. Now if you'll excuse me, I would like to get some sleep."

I pointed to the door. She glanced at it and then back at me. "You really don't get it, do you? I am not going anywhere. I am bound to you because you freed me. I owe you. And I want to thank you. But since you got me out, we might as well figure out who put me in there, because it was definitely somebody and I'd like to know who."

"No," I told her.

Okay, I should have said yes, and normally I would have. The me of six months ago would have. But I was not me from six months ago. I

25

was Paige Provey in the now, and this Paige Provey was tired of dealing with the whims of others.

"Look, I just need a good night's sleep, and everything will be better."

I strode over to the door, even though I knew she had slipped through my wall and a door wouldn't stop her if she wanted to get back in. But for the time being, I was just going to ignore that.

Anyway, I opened the front door and listened as crickets chirped and frogs croaked. "If you wouldn't mind please leaving. You don't have to go home, but you can't stay here, as they say."

She eyed me for a long moment. "Um, have you ever been told that you're delusional?"

"No, and I'm not about to be. Please." I pointed to the outside world. "And please stop bothering me."

Snow gave me a sad look that caused my heart to lurch before she slipped outside. I did not notice that where her feet should have been, she simply didn't have any.

All right, so I did, but I did my best to ignore it. First thing in the morning I would call my medical doctor and get a referral to a psychiatrist.

I needed one and bad.

With Snow gone from the cabin, I shut the door and locked it up tight. Then I checked to make sure the windows were also sealed, which they were.

When that was done, I rinsed out my coffee cup and headed into the bedroom.

Then stopped. Walked back to the kitchen and opened the drawers until I found what I was looking for—a big, sharp knife.

I pulled one out and stared at it. If Snow came back, it wouldn't hurt to have a weapon.

But then again, steel only worked on flesh and bone.

Sighing, I dropped the knife back into the drawer and headed to the bedroom.

But Snow had to be real. Okay, yes, it had appeared as if she'd stepped through the wall. Yet it must have been some sort of trick. I was sure of it. Walter was probably behind the whole thing. Yes, that was what was going on. Walter had hired Snow, and she was probably from

Hollywood and had some app on her phone that produced special effects.

That was why she didn't have feet and could glide through walls.

I shivered just thinking about it. But it was all a joke, a way for Walter to extort more money from me.

My phone pinged from the nightstand. If it was Walter, I would kill him.

It wasn't. This was much worse.

Madeleine: *How's the book coming?*

I groaned. "It's not, Madeleine. You'll probably end up firing me. The publishing company probably will, too. It's horrible."

But instead of typing, I decided to respond to her the next morning, when hopefully I would be feeling better. I pulled the covers over my head and fell into a deep sleep.

The next morning the sun was high when I got out of bed. The birds chirped and dew dripped from the tree leaves. It was a glorious morning.

"Ah, that's better," I said.

I had known that things would look clearer, sharper in the morning. They always did. After stretching and showering, I pulled on a pair of leggings and a T-shirt, deciding that today would be grocery shopping day and I would also get one page written of my book.

I had no idea what I would be writing about, but I'd figure it out—if it killed me.

"To think that I thought I was talking to an actual ghost. Pssh. Glad that nightmare's over."

I was making coffee when a voice came from behind me. "How'd you sleep?"

I screamed and whirled around, soup spoon in hand as a weapon. "What are you doing here? How'd you get in?"

Snow was sitting at the kitchen table, her chin propped in the cup of her hand like she was bored. "I told you, I can walk through walls. I'm dead. Like, I'm not alive. I haven't been alive in a long, long time. Ever since—"

"You were put into the book. I know. You said." I studied her. I'd already told her to leave. I'd already made it abundantly clear that I didn't want Snow in my life, that she needed to go get her own life, but here she was, seeking my help.

At some point I had to realize that she needed me. And that, maybe, I needed her, too.

"Okay, hold still," I told her. I walked over and raked my hand through her hair. I felt nothing. There was no hair. Then I did the same to her shoulder. Not only was she transparent, but she was also nothing more than air. "Stay there."

I walked outside and all around the cabin to make sure that there weren't any set lights or props that could help with the illusion. I wasn't born yesterday, you know?

I certainly didn't want to get taken for any kind of ride. After a few minutes I was satisfied that Snow wasn't being manufactured from outside the cabin.

"Great," I muttered to myself. "This is just great. When I should have been seeing ghosts, I wasn't, and now I am when I don't need to."

I strode back inside. She still sat at the table. I situated myself across from her and sighed. "Okay, tell me everything."

Snow slowly smiled. "Well, it all started in 1997."

CHAPTER 6

"*I* was living here, in Willow Lake," Snow explained.

It took all my concentration *not* to focus on the fact that the woman sitting across from me was mostly transparent.

"What happened?" I prodded.

She clutched the ghostly pearls around her neck. "Well, I was minding my own business, at home one day, when someone came to the door. I don't remember who, but I let them in, so I must've known them. And the next thing I knew, I was in the book, trapped."

"You don't remember anything else at all?"

"No. But do you think we can figure out who did this to me based on that?"

No. "Maybe?"

"You could perhaps talk to my next-door neighbor. Her name was Pam. She was the sweetest woman. She might know something."

"Okay, um, all right. Look, I'm just here for the summer, I'm not looking to start a true crime podcast or anything." Her expression fell. "Wait. I take that back. I'll do what I can to help you."

Snow's face lit up like a firework. "You will? Oh, thank you." She threw her arms around my neck and I supposed you could say that she hugged me, but it felt like I was being wrapped up in spider silk. I only felt the barest tickle.

"No need to get carried away," I told her.

Snow sniffled and nodded.

Hoping that I hadn't hurt her feelings, I said, "Well, I need to get into town and buy some groceries."

"I'll come," she said.

I held up my hand in a stop position. "No, no. That's okay. I can do it myself. Besides, if people see me talking to the air, they're going to think that I'm, well, um…"

"Crazy?"

"That's the word." I grabbed my purse and ran my fingers through my hair, hoping that not one strand was out of place. "I'll be back. See you soon."

As soon as I was out the door, I pressed my back to it and exhaled. What in the world was going on? How could I see her? She was a ghost. A ghost! I didn't want to keep freaking out in front of Snow as that could cut deeply into her confidence, but my heart was thundering.

How was I seeing a ghost?

Maybe it had to do with being hit on the head with the book that she'd fallen out of it. Okay. *Get yourself together, Paige.* It was only one ghost. I could only see Snow. It wasn't like I could now see armies of spirits.

I exhaled and felt better. That was true. I only saw Snow.

Whew. Life was good.

Now it was time to get some food.

My phone rang while I was in the car. I pressed the Bluetooth. "Hello?"

"It's Madeleine."

Crap. If I'd known my agent was going to be on the other line, I would've evaded the call. "It's so great to talk to you. How're things going?"

"Fine, darling. Fine. Listen, I'm calling to find out how the book is going. Usually by this time, you're sending me pages. What've you got?"

"Oh, I'm hard at work," I lied. "Really, this one is coming fast and furious."

"You're lying."

I scoffed. "You don't know that."

"Yes, I do. I've been working with you for over ten years. When you have pages, I have them. This is the first time in all those years that I haven't seen one word."

"I'm trying to come up with something," I admitted.

"Darling, you've had trauma. Are you at the lake like you promised?"

"Yes. I am."

"Are you relaxing?"

Only if you counted seeing ghosts as relaxing. "I'm trying to."

"Good. The pages will come. The ideas will spring forward. I've never once been in the country and not been rejuvenated. Take your time. Read some books. But know that I've got to show the publisher something soon. Your editor is calling. Not being pushy, just asking how the book's coming. I don't have to tell you that a lot is riding on this."

"No, you don't." My stomach knotted nervously. "Of course you don't. I know that."

"This book could redeem you, or it could…"

Put the final nail in my coffin? Madeleine didn't say it, but I knew that was what she was thinking. "I got it. I'm working. I'll have pages to you soon."

"Please do."

She hung up and I felt worse than I had before. Now I had a ghost who wanted help and my agent was pestering me for a book that I didn't have, that I had no idea how to write.

But all was good. I would figure things out. I always did. Anyway, by the time that I finished the phone call, I'd reached the outskirts of town.

Willow Lake was the epitome of small-town charming. There was a grocery store at the end of Main Street and lots of shops that lined both sides of the road—clothing boutiques, an art gallery, antique shops—all the basics, as well as several local restaurants.

As this was prime lake season, the Wilson's Grocery Store parking lot was packed.

I got out and headed inside. I grabbed a buggy from a line and sighed as the cool air-conditioning swept down my back. It was only morning, and the humidity was already making me sweat. That's just how summer in the South was, I supposed.

"Good morning," said the greeter.

"Good morning." I glanced up to smile and gasped. The greeter's normal human head had been replaced by what looked like a troll's noggin—knotted skin, pointy ears, sharp teeth and all. Fear bolted down my spine. The urge to run overcame me, but I took a deep breath and said in a teasing voice, "You almost had me, there. Y'all gearing up for Halloween early this year?"

"Ma'am?" he asked.

"The mask." I pointed to his face. "It's a good one. You had me." I shook my head and pushed my buggy along.

First thing I needed was to hit the deli for sandwich meat. No one stood behind the counter, and there was a bell to ring for service, so I tapped it.

"Yes, can I help you?"

I turned to greet the woman who was going to slice my meat and yelped. Her face was covered in fur as if she had that terrible disease that affected those two boys who'd been dubbed "the werewolf boys"—hirsutism, I think it was called, when a person's hair growth was out of control.

"I'm so sorry," I apologized. "I just…um…had a pain in my rear end. It shot all the way to my spine, and I thought that I was going to keel over."

I couldn't exactly tell the nice woman smiling at me that her face had scared the living daylights out of me, now could I?

"What would you like?" she asked, unfazed.

"A pound of turkey meat," I told her.

While she was slicing, I took a moment to give myself a pep talk.

Paige, you have got to pull it together. I couldn't keep freaking out when I saw people. That simply wouldn't do. I had to keep myself in line, not lose it.

The deli worker gave me the meat, and I thanked her, making sure to look her in the eyes instead of gazing at the fur that covered her face…and neck…and arms.

Okay, so that was a lot of hair. I prayed none of it dusted my meat.

I thanked her again and finished up my list. While I walked around, I noticed other workers who looked like the troll and who were also hairy. Were the hairy people related? Was the grocery store really big on equal opportunity? If so, good for them.

When my basket was full, I spotted one checkout line open, so I beelined for it.

"Did you find everything to your satisfaction?" the girl behind the register asked.

"Yes, I did, thank you. Though I was wondering what's going on? Are y'all celebrating Halloween early or something?"

"What do you mean?"

I placed the last of my packages on the moving belt and faced her. "Well, there are all those folks with the troll masks on, and I think it's great that the management hired all those folks with hirsutism. You know, it's got to be hard for them to find jobs."

"I'm not sure I understand what you mean," she said.

Her words were surprising, but what was more shocking was that her canines were incredibly long, like at least an inch, and very, very pointy, almost like she was a—

That was ridiculous. This woman wasn't a vampire.

I laughed feebly at her response that she didn't understand what I meant. "Oh, you know. Everyone here is dressed up for Halloween. Even you've got those long vampire teeth."

Her eyes widened and she quickly covered her mouth. In fact, she covered her mouth for the entire time, hurrying to finish the transaction. I paid her and headed out, embarrassed by my callous behavior.

Obviously her extra-long teeth made her uncomfortable, and I had to go and highlight them.

I was such a jerk.

I hustled to my car and placed the groceries in back. As I came around front, I spotted the grocery store sign. Where at first I'd thought it said Wilson's Grocery, I realized that wasn't what was written on the sign at all. The W had thrown me, but I realized that the name was completely different.

It wasn't Wilson's Grocery. It was Werewolf's Grocery.

My heart nearly skidded to a stop. I was so shocked that I stared again at the sign, but it didn't change. In fact, I took the time to read the names of the other stores. The ACE Hardware place was called Troll Brother's Hardware. The antique shop was Bloodsucking Baubles; even the busy restaurant's name was Ghoul's Delights instead of Gertrude's Delights.

I felt weak. My heart was racing; sweat poured from my forehead. What was going on?

"Are you all right?" came a voice.

I glanced up to see Jason Momoa himself, Grim, striding toward me with a scowl on his face. *A scowl.* Couldn't he even ask a person if they were okay without looking like a top model?

"Yes, I'm fine," I snapped.

"You don't look fine. You look like you've seen a ghost."

I threw my hands in the air. "A ghost! A vampire! A troll! I think that I've even seen a werewolf."

His eyes widened in alarm. "Look, why don't you and I go chat somewhere? Your name's Paige, right?"

"Why do you want to chat with me? So that you can convince me that I'm crazy? Is there something in the water here? I'm losing my mind; I know it."

He stepped toward me. "Maybe we should—"

"I'm getting out of here. I don't know what's going on, but this is too much for me."

Before he could say another word, I got into my SUV and gunned it toward the road.

"You are not going crazy," I said to myself as I bounded toward the cabin. "I am not nuts. I know what I saw. This town, it isn't like I remember."

That cashier, had she been a vampire? It made sense, seeing as she'd covered her mouth. She wasn't embarrassed. She was hiding her true identity.

Oh God. I was losing my mind. There was no such thing as vampires. Or werewolves. Or trolls. Or any of it.

I would leave. I was already cracking up, thinking that I'd spent time talking to a ghost. I would return to the cabin, pack my things, demand Patricia give me a refund and head out.

It would work.

I reached the cabin in record time and raced into the house. There wasn't much in the living room for me to pack up—my computer, my coffee. That was it. I threw them into a box and put them in my car. Next thing was my clothes. I raced into the bedroom and screamed.

There, lying on my bed, lay Walter. He wasn't moving. He couldn't, in fact. The only thing that he could do was stare at the ceiling because someone had rammed a knife through his heart.

Footsteps sounded behind me. I turned around to see a young deputy in a blue shirt with a gun on his belt, looming in the doorway. He had shaggy brown hair and a lanky build. He was handsome but young, and looked a little green behind the ears.

He wiped a hand across his mouth. "We got a call about a domestic disturbance out here." He peeked over my shoulder. "I'd say that disturbance went pretty wrong. Why don't you tell me why you killed him?"

My jaw dropped. "But I'm innocent. I just walked in and found him like this."

He smirked. "You can tell me everything down at the station."

With that, he pulled out a pair of handcuffs and snapped them onto my wrists.

Maybe he wasn't as green as I'd thought.

CHAPTER 7

"*I*'m telling you that I had nothing to do with it, uh, Officer Cowan," I said, reading the name off his badge. "I swear that I just arrived home and he was dead. I was about to call you. Or someone." He started to drag me toward the door, but I pushed in my heels. "Look, will you please just listen to me? Will you stop for one second?"

"What's going on here?"

I glanced up to see Grim in my cabin. What in the world was he doing here?

Officer Cowan immediately dropped his hands from my cuffs. "Oh, Grim, sir, I was just… There's a dead man in her bedroom, and I got a call about loud noises coming from here. When I arrived, this woman was standing over the body."

"Because I'd just gotten home," I snapped. "You saw me," I said to Grim. (Why I was hoping he would help, I didn't know. All he'd been to me up until this point was a pain in my rear end). "We were at the grocery store together. Or at least the parking lot. I was coming back here to pack up and leave this place—to get the heck out—and then I found my ex-husband in my bed with a knife in his chest."

I stopped, realizing that I was screaming, which probably didn't look good for me. Grim glanced at Cowan. "She's right; I did just see her at the grocery store."

"An alibi," Cowan murmured.

"I can hear you," I told him. "I'm not deaf. Just handcuffed."

Grim nodded. "Until we know further, question her and that's it."

Who was this Grim guy? He wasn't even dressed like an officer.

"But...?"

"Do it," Grim said.

Cowan reluctantly unlocked my cuffs. I made sure to rub my wrists like they always did in the movies so that Cowan would know he'd made my skin tender.

I placed my hands on my hips. "Now. I told you everything. I came home and found him dead. I hadn't been gone long at all, just to get groceries. That's all I know."

Cowan grabbed his walkie-talkie. "I need to call this in. Stay put."

Where else would I go? My ex was dead, so clearly I wouldn't be leaving anytime soon.

Grim gave Cowan a nod. "I'll wait until backup comes."

Cowan walked outside, leaving me and Grim alone. As much as I didn't want to do it, I felt the need to say to him, "Thank you."

He nodded.

That was it.

Had he been brought up in a barn? Like, who responded that way when someone thanked him? Maybe if I stroked his ego a bit more, he'd be nicer.

"Wow, you must have some pull with the police."

"Let's just say I...help them."

Oh. "I hadn't realized that."

"That's because you were too busy pushing my backpack off your side of the bar."

Right. Stick foot in mouth? Check. "Listen, I'm sorry about that, but it was on my side of the space." He didn't say anything. Okay, talking to him was going to be harder than I thought. "So, um, what do you do for the police?"

"Special things."

As if that answered the question. "Sounds exciting. I'm a writer. I love hearing details of people's lives."

"That must be nice."

Heat flamed on my neck. He was being so difficult. It didn't help that his cheeks had been cut by diamonds and that his silver eyes were piercing. Not that I had noticed.

"How old are you?" he asked.

What? How had we gotten to my age? "Thirty-nine."

Total lie. I was forty-three, but he didn't need to know that.

"Well, Paige," he snarled, "I would figure that by your age if a person wants to tell you about themself, they'll freely give that information, and you pestering them with questions isn't going to change anyone's mind about how much they tell you."

My entire head was on fire, I was so embarrassed. But I wasn't going to let this glorified surfer boy have the last say.

"Pester? There was no pestering involved. And I suggest," I said, standing up on my tiptoes and leaning in (which made his eyes flare in surprise), "that the next time you want to play rescue and come to my aid, you bring me a coffee. I drink it black. Sometimes with cream. But I have to be in the mood."

I didn't wait for his reply, because I walked away as Officer Cowan was returning from his call.

A FEW MINUTES later Grim left and the cabin was swarming with police officers. I was back with Cowan, explaining what had happened.

"I came back here—the groceries are still in my car. I'm sure the milk is ruined by now, but anyway. Not important. And I found Walter dead."

Cowan tapped the end of his pen on a pad of paper. "Had he been here?"

I raked my fingers through my hair in frustration. "No. I don't know how he got in. I came back and there he was."

Cowan smirked. I could tell he had a real doozy of a question lined up for me. "And what was your relationship like with the deceased?"

Bad? Was that a good answer? "Strained. We got divorced a little over six months ago."

"Usually when folks get divorced, they don't have much to do with one another after unless there was money involved."

I stared at him coldly. "There was. Mine."

"Huh." Cowan scratched his head as if he was trying to wrap his mind around that. "Your money?"

I sighed. "Yes. I am—*was* a successful author."

"Was?"

"Yes. I was canceled."

He blinked. "Canceled?"

Was no one aware of this term? Frustrated, I nearly shouted, "Yes, canceled. My life destroyed. I'm trolled constantly on the Internet. People wanted me dead. They said I was horrible and that I should take a dirt nap."

"A dirt nap?"

I rolled my eyes. "Yes, it means to die. Anyway, I paid Walter alimony, but he took a lot of the cash in the divorce. There wasn't much left. That's why I'm here." I gestured toward the cabin. "So that I can come up with my next brilliant idea and get paid," I added sarcastically.

"Is it really that easy to come up with a brilliant idea?" His tone was so genuine that it was impossible to bite his head off for asking such a moronic question.

"No, it isn't," I confessed. "If I could pop brilliance out like puppies, I'd be doing great. But I'm not."

"Oh, you should meet my mom. She can pop out some puppies."

I blinked, totally confused by his statement. The only thing I could come up with was, "Well, that's good to know. If I'm ever in the market for—what kind of dogs does she breed?"

"Wolves."

I balked. "Is that legal?"

He frowned. "You don't need a permit, if that's what you're asking."

What kind of crazy place was this? Owning wolves usually required having an exotic pet permit. I'd researched that for a book, so I knew it. What was Officer Cowan talking about?

"Oh, I thought you needed one," I murmured.

"Not for this type of wolf," he informed me.

Okay then. "Anyway, yes, Walter got alimony from me."

"Was that something you generally argued about? Neighbors heard arguing coming from here."

"What neighbors?" I spun around but saw nothing but trees and lake. "I haven't seen any."

Cowan pointed up the road. "Mrs. Butts is up the way. She wears a hearing aid and swears that she can hear two counties away." He chuckled. "She wouldn't be lying, either, because if anyone can tell when the train's about to run through town, it's her. She always hears it when no one else can."

"Well, if Walter was arguing with someone, it wasn't me. I had nothing to do with it. Like I said, I had just come back."

"So why would he have been here? To collect money?"

This conversation was getting a little too close for comfort. "Yes, probably. I ran into him last night."

Cowan arched his ridiculously sculpted eyebrows. Did he wax? Pluck? No, I bet that he got them threaded. There was that kind of precision to how he was missing any and all stray hairs. Heck, his brows looked better than mine.

"And what happened last night?" he asked.

Oh crap. "Well, he tracked me down at the grill—"

"Was Ferguson working?"

"Yep, he was." What did that have to do with my case? "He's a good bartender."

"Aw, just the best. Don't you love him? Great bedside manner. I always tell him that if he'd gone into the medical field, he would've made a great doctor. Lots of precision."

Alrighty then. "Walter met up with me and asked for his money. I told him the truth—that I'm broke and that I need to sell my next book before I can give him anything."

"Cowan," one of the deputies said.

"Yeah?"

"I've got something."

"Now?" Cowan asked. "Can't you see I'm in the middle of this interview?"

"It'll only take a sec."

Cowan smiled. "Be right back. Don't move, or I'll be forced to put those handcuffs on you."

"Don't you worry," I assured him. "I'll be right here."

Cowan moved off to talk to the deputy, and I took a moment to study the landscape. I couldn't see another house for the thick trees. Who was this Mrs. Butts that she'd heard something? How could she possibly have heard anything? They must've been really shouting it up for the sound to move through the forest.

After a moment Cowan returned. His brow was furrowed in a very serious expression.

"Everything okay?" I asked.

"Not really. It seems you forgot an important detail in your conversation with Walter."

"What was that?"

"That you told him you'd kill him."

My stomach dropped. "Right. Well, you know how it is in the heat of an argument—people say things that they don't mean. Obviously I wasn't going to kill him. At one point I married him."

"Ma'am," he said stiffly, "you'd be surprised how many spouses kill their...um...spouses."

"Well, he wasn't my spouse," I corrected.

"They also kill ex-spouses."

Darn it. I couldn't win here. "Look," I said, throwing everything I had into the conversation. "I know that this appears bad. Trust me, I do. But you've got to believe me. I had nothing to do with his murder. I have an alibi. That big, huge, handsome man—what's his name? Grim?"

"Yeah, Grim." Cowan clicked his tongue. "He is handsome, isn't he? I tell you, I never want to double date with him again. Made that mistake once, and my girl ended up fawning all over him by the time the night was over."

"Oh? So he has a girlfriend? Not that I'm interested. I mean, not that I want to know." I chuckled nervously. "I just thought since you said 'girlfriend' that he probably had one."

"Nope, Grim's single, much to the dismay of all the women in town. He's sworn off love, he says." Cowan leaned forward. "But between you and me, I think he just hasn't met the right gal. Got burned once in love."

"Oh, she break his heart?"

"No, I mean literally. She set him on fire."

"Fire?" My jaw dropped. "You're kidding."

"Wish I was. But no."

I exhaled a gust of air. "What kind of psycho sets a man on fire?"

"Um, anyway." Cowan rubbed the back of his neck. "Look, back to your conversation with your husband."

"Ex-husband."

"Right. You seem like a nice woman and all, but given the fact that you told him you'd kill him, it looks like—"

"Cowan, we got a match on the prints found on the knife." It was the same deputy who'd pulled him aside earlier.

"Great," I said, relieved. "Now y'all can go find the actual murderer."

Cowan looked at the sheet of paper the deputy handed him. "Um, not so fast, Ms. Provey." His gaze locked on mine. "It appears that your prints were found all over the murder weapon."

CHAPTER 8

"That's because I picked up the knife last night. I was scared. Thought that someone was lurking around outside." Like a ghost. "Look, I told you that I don't know anything about Walter's murder. I found him dead. You can grill me until I pass out, but I didn't do this. I swear."

Cowan looked at me skeptically.

After finding my prints on the knife, Cowan had taken me down to the station for questioning. But there hadn't been anything for them to find because I was innocent.

"Please," I pleaded. "I know this looks bad, but I had nothing to do with it."

"Ms. Provey, if you would just like to admit to killing Walter, then we could move things along."

I dropped my face into my hands. My life had gone from bad to worse in five minutes. "I had nothing to do with it. I know that I'm an outsider and that you don't know me. But I wouldn't kill anybody."

A knock came from the door. "Excuse me," Cowan said. He pushed a box of tissues closer to me. "In case you start crying." It took everything I had not to shoot him a dark look. But he returned a few minutes later, and when he did, the officer said, "Looks like you can go. For now. Okay?"

"What? You're releasing me?"

"For a little while. Now, be good out there. We may interview you again." He placed his hands on his hips and continued in a chastising voice, "Don't make me have to come out there and get you. Seems that an important detail was discovered. So like I said, for now you're free to go."

I couldn't get out of the station fast enough. As I made my way through the bullpen, I spotted a female police officer with wings sprouting from her back.

I stopped and stared, having nearly forgotten about Werewolf Grocery and the other monster places that I'd seen.

"Ms. Provey," Cowan said loudly from the end of the corridor.

I turned around and smiled. "Yes?"

"Be sure not to leave town. That would look very bad for you."

I motioned to the winged fairy. "Halloween called. It wants its holiday back."

With that, I stormed from the building and stepped outside, only to realize that I had no way to get home.

"Crap," I fumed. "What am I supposed to do now?"

I sure as heck wasn't going back inside the police station to beg a ride from Officer Cowan. He'd probably spend five minutes discussing the merits of electric versus gasoline vehicles.

I did not have the interest in me to do that.

While I stood huffing and puffing, a big Suburban pulled up. The windows were tinted black, and I was wondering if a movie star had rolled into town when a window buzzed down.

"Need a ride?" Ferguson asked.

I exhaled a gust of air in relief. "Yes, thank goodness. You showed up at just the right time." I smiled at him. "You don't mind driving out to the lake, do you?"

"Lass, this whole town's a lake," he said in his thick brogue. "Tell me where you live, and I'll get you there."

Now I hadn't seen Ferguson out from behind the bar, but when I climbed inside, the hairs on the back of my neck prickled to attention.

There was a pair of fake legs and shoes on the brake and accelerator. Ferguson's own feet dangled from the seat. After I clicked in my belt, he pushed his feet into the false legs, and we started moving down the road.

I had no idea what to say. Never in my life had I seen a person wearing false feet. Why, Ferguson must've only been about three feet tall. I wasn't judging, though. From all the weirdness that I'd seen in one day, this was nothing.

"You didn't get robbed, did you?" he asked.

"What?"

"The police station. You were standing outside it."

"Oh, that. Right. Um, no. My ex-husband wound up murdered. In my bed." Probably shouldn't have told him any of that. It more than likely wasn't good for our relationship—you know, the bonding part of it and all—but for some reason I didn't care. "I didn't do it, though. Someone else did."

He cocked a brow. "You say he was found dead?"

"At the cabin I'm staying in. Of all the bad luck, right?"

"I'm sorry," he said soberly.

"Walter was a peeping Tom."

"Excuse me?"

I sighed. "Never mind." I pointed to a sign for Witch's Brew, a coffee shop. "Ferguson, what's going on in town? Last time I was here, all the stores had normal names, but now it's Werewolf Grocery and Witch's Brew, and I swear half the town is dressed up for Halloween. Have I missed some memo?"

I turned to eye him, but his gaze darted to the windshield. "I'm not sure I know what you're talking about."

"Maybe I just have a brain tumor."

"Er, um, I don't think that's it."

We rode in silence the rest of the way. I directed him down my dirt road, and when I hopped out, Ferguson plucked his real feet from the fake ones. My gaze immediately darted to his legs.

His eyes tracked mine, and he quickly shoved his feet back into the fake legs. "Well, I'll be seeing you," he said.

"Thank you. Can I pay you for the ride?"

But before I heard his answer, the door slammed shut as if by a fierce wind and the Suburban's tires spit gravel as Ferguson darted off, away from me.

"What is going on in this town?" Ferguson had acted strangely when I saw his fake legs, as if I wasn't supposed to have spotted them. But he'd pulled his feet out. What was the deal?

"Oh, the sooner I can get out of this town, the better," I said.

But wait. How would I do that? I was under suspicion of murder, and I didn't have money for an attorney. I was trapped in Willow Lake until my name was cleared and they found the real killer.

The real killer. What real killer?

"Where've you been?"

Snow floated up to me.

Great. Just what I needed. A ghost. I must have been suffering from delusions. Maybe I had schizophrenia, and it had simply gone undiagnosed all these years.

The police were gone from the cabin, having taken away Walter's body and the mattress too, I hoped.

To Snow I said, "I've been at the police station. Do you know that my ex-husband was killed in the cabin? Did you see him?"

Oh my gosh. Had she? What if Snow had seen what happened? She could save my skin on this.

Snow grimaced. "I saw the body, yes. I was hoping that was an illusion."

"Illusion? Ha! I'm the one suffering from illusions and delusions and all the *usions*. I'm talking to a ghost, and this town has undergone some sort of strange Halloween transformation. I'm seeing ghouls and vampires and maybe even werewolves. Wait. No. I'm not going there. Look—and I can't believe that I'm even asking this, but—did you see something? Do you know why Walter was here? Who he was with? Do you know anything?"

Snow withered. I mean, even though she was a ghost, I actually felt bad for her. "I didn't see anything. I'm sorry."

I ran my fingers through my hair. "It's okay. I shouldn't have put all of that on you."

I'd started to go inside when Snow said, "Wait."

"Yes?"

"I may have heard something."

"What was that?"

"Kissing sounds," Snow said.

My jaw dropped. "What? Kissing sounds? You heard Walter kissing someone in the cabin that I'm staying in?"

Wouldn't it just figure that my scourge of an ex-husband would have broken into my cabin and then started making out with the woman who killed him? At this point nothing would have surprised me.

Snow nodded. "I definitely heard kissing. I think there might even be a butt print in the kitchen."

My jaw dropped. "A butt print? What makes you say that?"

She leaned in conspiratorially. "Because I heard him say, let me put you on the counter."

A butt print! I had no idea if it would help, but I raced into the cabin. "Let me see."

"I'll follow."

I ran into the kitchen, which looked completely normal, as if nothing had ever happened. My phone dinged in my pocket, and I pulled it out to see a text from Madeleine.

Just checking in, darling. All going well?

My stomach knotted just thinking about how I would explain this to my agent. *Well, Madeleine, it's not going so great. Walter showed up and was found dead in my bed. Also this entire town has gone crazy. So there's that...*

But the light on my phone gave me an idea. I punched on the flashlight and washed the phone up and down the counter. "Come on, butt print. If we can match your butt to someone else's, we'll be doing great."

"Do you see it?" Snow asked from beside me.

"Not yet."

I glanced around but didn't see a print. My hopes sank. "It's not here. Nothing's here."

"Wait." Snow pointed to the desk, the one that my computer sat on. "What's this?"

I hovered the phone over my computer and, sure enough, on top of my laptop sat the imprint of a bottom crack.

Oh. My. Gosh.

If I hadn't wanted Walter dead before, I did now. He had let some slimy hussy sit on top of my computer. I might have to burn it. I might have to throw it away and never look back.

"That's evidence," Snow pointed out.

Unfortunately she was right. "It doesn't look like a very big butt print."

"That is a small butt," she concurred. "A tiny woman with probably one of those great figures—you know the kind; they have three kids and still look Hollywood amazing."

I knew the kind. I was childless, but that didn't mean I hadn't observed what happened to women's bodies after they had kids. Plenty of times I got trapped listening as my friends complained about how hard it was to get back into shape after giving birth.

"You're right. This is the butt of someone who works out. I'm taking a picture. The police could use this as evidence."

Snow tsked. "Do you really think the police are going to listen when you tell them that you have an imprint of the killer's butt? They'll think you sat on your own laptop naked and then took a picture."

I laughed. "But why would I... Oh, right. So that they wouldn't think I was guilty." She had a point—a really, really good point. "Well, I'm at least going to take a picture."

I snapped several photos. "Well, that's done. Let's see if there were any clues left in the bedroom."

The mattress had been confiscated, which was fine by me. The room itself was barren of any more clues.

"Well, we tried," Snow said.

"Yep. Looks like I need a new mattress." I googled a local mattress place and made arrangements for a new one to be delivered later that afternoon. There were plenty of sheets in the closet, so at least I had that going for me.

It was after I got off the phone that something struck me. "Did you hear Walter arguing with someone?"

She opened the fridge. "Empty."

"Oh my gosh, the groceries!"

I ran outside and pulled out what I'd bought that morning. The milk was ruined, but the rest of it was salvageable. I stocked the fridge while Snow inspected my cache.

"No cheese?"

"You can't eat. You're dead."

She shrugged. "Minor inconvenience, but no, I didn't hear any arguing."

"Well, according to the police, one of the neighbors did."

Snow's eyes sparkled. "Are you thinking what I'm thinking? That we need some cheese?"

"No. I'm thinking that I need to pay this neighbor a visit, starting right now."

CHAPTER 9

The sun was setting as Snow and I walked toward my nearest neighbor's house. Honestly I had no idea exactly where she lived, but Cowan had pointed north, so that was the way we were walking.

Or I was walking. Snow floated.

"What I wouldn't give to be able to have a Little Debbie treat," Snow said. "Or hear Ace of Base again."

I did a double take. "Ace of Base?"

"Yeah, you know—" She burst into song. "'I saw the sign and it opened up my eyes and I am happy now living without you.'"

"Oh, that tune brings back memories. I was in college when it came out. Or end of high school or something. I loved it. I used to sing it with my sister," I mused.

Snow's brows lifted. "You have a sister?"

"Yes, and trust me, she is nothing like me. She lives…a ways away."

"Oh, you're not close."

Not close was putting it nicely. Cammie and I were polar opposites. She had been married and divorced three times, lived in a trailer park, and I only heard from her when she needed money.

"Well, we're different. Let's just put it that way."

"She the black sheep of the family?" Snow leaned over as if we were in on a secret. "You can tell me. I promise not to blab."

I hooted with laughter. "Who are you going to tell? You're dead."

"That is unfortunately very true. Oh, look. We're here."

Indeed we were. The lake cabin was constructed of brown logs. There were flower boxes lining the windows and a beautiful bed of geraniums in the front. A flag with a pink camellia had been fastened to the porch, and it whipped in the wind.

"What a nice little place," I mused. "The woman who lives here must be the sweetest thin—"

"If you take one more step, I'll blow your head off." On the porch stood a woman holding a shotgun leveled at my head. "Put your hands up."

I did as she said. Snow didn't. How lucky she was not to be seen. The sweet little thing on the front porch—my *neighbor* who'd planted all those beautiful flowers—had a pinched-up little face, a squat body and looked about one hundred and three.

"Hi," I said, putting on my friendliest sounding voice. "I'm your neighbor, Paige Provey?"

"Are you asking me if you're my neighbor?"

My voice had risen on the last word into a question. "Sorry. No. I'm just nervous because you're pointing a lethal weapon at my head."

She didn't take the hint and drop the barrel. Instead she just kept it trained on my face. I couldn't afford plastic surgery if she shot me, that was how broke I was.

"My name's Paige Provey. I'm renting the cabin down the road. The police told me that you heard arguing today."

"You come up here to kill me like you did to your husband?"

I clenched my teeth in anger. "*Ex*-husband. He was my ex. We'd been divorced awhile."

"Then why'd you kill him?"

"I didn't kill him! And how do you know so much?"

"News travels fast in this here town. Plus I can hear good."

"Great. That's why I'm here. I was wondering if you'd heard anything that could help me find Walter's killer. Because I didn't do it."

She stared at me with beady eyes for a long moment. It felt like she was scanning my soul for something. "Come on up," she relented. "I'll tell you what I know."

I sighed with relief. "Thank goodness."

I climbed up the stairs, and when I got there, I saw that the woman wasn't holding a shotgun. She was holding a stick instead.

I frowned. "From down there, on the ground, that looked like a shotgun. But it's not."

She didn't say anything. Only led me inside. If the outside had been charming, the inside was downright mystical. All types of flowers were potted everywhere, the room springing with color. It was like stepping inside a hothouse, only not nearly so muggy.

"My name's Estelle. Have a seat, Paige."

I sat while Snow hovered around, inspecting the place. Whew. I was glad that Estelle couldn't see Snow, because the way that the ghost was snooping in her house was certainly not polite.

"Would you like some tea?" Estelle asked.

"Yes, please." She opened a door in the coffee table and pulled out a tea set. My eyes nearly bugged from my head. "Oh, wow. That was like magic."

Estelle pursed her lips.

I laughed nervously for some odd reason. "Do you always store tea there?"

"Only when guests are coming. I heard you a mile off."

"Right. You can hear well. That's what Cowan told me," I said, taking a glass. "That's why I'm here."

"So you said. You want to know what I heard, right? I'm the one who called in the arguing. Sounded like a pretty bad domestic disturbance down there."

I leaned forward in my chair. "That's what I was wondering. Did you catch a name or recognize the voice of the woman?"

"What do I look like, a psychic?"

I smiled. "No. I just thought maybe you knew something."

I'd already ruled out that Estelle had anything to do with Walter's murder. Her bottom was way too large to have made the small imprint on my computer.

Not that I was fat-shaming. I certainly wasn't. It was just that, well, she was big-bottomed. There. I'd said it.

Estelle eyed me through her thick glasses. "I tell you what I know—that man was arguing with a woman whose voice sounded a lot like yours."

"Mine?" I said, taken back. "How could it have sounded like mine?"

"How should I know? All I know is that it did. So if you didn't have anything to do with it, then the person who did sounded a lot like you."

"Well, that doesn't sound..." Possible? Was I going to say that? A day ago I wouldn't have thought it possible to talk to a ghost, but there was Snow, walking around Estelle's house, and the old woman didn't even see her.

So what was actually possible anymore?

Estelle pulled a deck of cards from the coffee table's cabinet. "Want to play Phase 10?"

"Um...?"

She sensed my hesitation, because Estelle said, "Tell you what—you play a game with me, and I might be able to tell you a little more about what I know about your ex-husband's death."

"You know more?"

"Maybe. That's for you to find out."

Estelle was a much more weaselly old woman than she was comforting-grandmother material. "Okay, I'll play with you. Just one game," I told her sternly.

She smiled as if knowing a secret that I didn't. Estella shuffled the cards and we began.

Two hours later we were still playing. From the corner Snow yawned. "I'm tired. So I'm going home. See you later."

Without another word, she slipped through the wall and disappeared from sight. "How long have we been at this?" I asked.

"Oh, I don't know. A little while now."

"I think that we've played our one game and you owe me the information that you were going to give me earlier. Remember when you said that you could tell me something else?"

"Oh, did I say that?" Estelle said, looking surprised. "Are you sure?"

"I'm sure. Now what is it? What other information do you have?"

"Well"—she smacked her lips—"seems to me that before I heard your voice, there was someone else's voice that I heard."

I leaned in. This was news. This was good. This was something that

53

Estelle should have told me two hours ago. But I wasn't going to argue. Better late than never, I often said.

"Whose voice did you hear?"

Estelle smacked her lips. "I'm going to tell you this, but you didn't hear it from me. I don't know a thing, you understand?"

"Of course. Mum's the word." I made a big show of zipping my lips with my finger. "I won't tell a soul. Now. Whose voice was it?"

She squinted at me. "You sure that you're not going to say anything?"

"Totally promise. Absolutely. Not one word." Would she just tell me already? "If you had a Bible, I would place my hand on that. I won't tell a soul who I heard it from."

She opened the coffee table doors again and pulled out a Bible.

"Wow, you sure do have a lot stored in there."

Estelle ignored my question and held out the Bible. "Swear it."

So I laid my hand on the book. "I promise not to say who I got this information from."

She nodded, seeming satisfied. After tucking the Bible away, Estelle told me, "I know that I wasn't wrong about the voice. I've been hearing that voice for years. Heard Walter, too. Heard him talking to her."

It was a her? Maybe I could have a butt-print match! Then I'd be able to clear my name with the police. "Who was it?"

"It was a voice that I know in my sleep, one I've heard a thousand times."

Was Estelle milking this or what?

"I know it like the back of my hand," she continued.

"I'm beginning to think you don't know it at all. That's why you're making such a big deal about this."

"Nonsense. I just like the attention."

I rolled my eyes. "Okay. You've got my full attention. Now. Who was it?"

She arched forward and the dim light in the room made her eyes look like fire was dancing in them. She pulled her lips back into a sneer. "It was Patricia, your landlady."

Well, that was an interesting development.

CHAPTER 10

*I*t was dark when I set out for home. Estelle had kept me playing cards later than expected. I wasn't much of a player, but slapping cards down against Estelle had been fun.

Who was I becoming? I used to go on morning talk shows, and here I was being accused of murder and playing card games with a woman old enough to be my mother, if not my grandmother.

But that was neither here nor there.

I turned on the flashlight app on my phone and focused the beam on the dirt road in front of me.

I stopped. A dark shape like a blob was situated squarely in the middle of the road. I blinked to make sure that I was seeing it correctly, and yes, there was indeed an inky form taking up space where there shouldn't have been anything except Alabama red clay.

"What are you?" I whispered.

"What are you?" the spot repeated.

A chill swept down my spine. The thing could talk, but the voice was tinny, foreign sounding—not human.

I bit down the bile surging up the back of my throat. I had to stop freaking myself out. There were no such things as vampires. There were no such things as trolls. And there certainly were no such things as dark inky spots that could talk.

"Okay," I huffed.

"*Okay*," it repeated, still in that same strange voice.

I made a move to go around the creature, but it mimicked my motion, cutting me off from the road.

That was the point when fear started trickling into my thoughts. Maybe it should have crept in a bit sooner, but nope, that sucker was waiting until what I saw actually frightened me.

Perhaps reasoning with it would work. "Look, I need to get home, so if you'll excuse me."

"*Look, I need to get home, so if you'll excuse me,*" it mimicked.

Just as I was contemplating my next move, the thing started chittering. It sounded like a nest of bats calling to one another.

The fine hairs on the back of my neck soldiered to attention. Whatever it was, I had the feeling that I was in deep, dark trouble.

I ran, darting past the black spot and racing toward my house. Darn it! Estelle's had been right behind me. Why hadn't I just turned around and ran back there?

Because I hadn't wanted to turn my back on it, was why. Of course, now my back was to it, and I could hear it crashing through the leaves and trees as it made its way toward me.

All I had to do was reach the cabin. That was it. If I could just reach the cabi—

Something grabbed hold of my foot, and the next thing that I knew, I was facedown in the dirt, spitting out pebbles and dust particles that had been sucked into my mouth.

I whipped around and shone the light up. The creature had me by the foot. It smelled like death, and there was a slit in its face where its mouth would have been. The slit parted, revealing sharp teeth. I was staring into the devil's mouth, so evil was the grin.

The jaws opened and all I could think was that I wanted to be saved, that I wanted to be free, that I wanted the thing to leave me alone.

A green rope, seemingly coming from nowhere and yet everywhere at the same time, wrapped around the creature. It coiled around the thing's right arm. Then another rope grabbed its left arm.

The creature howled as it was dragged up and away from me. I scurried back in the dirt, pushing myself to standing and watched as the ropes—which weren't ropes at all, they were ivy vines—continued to curl around the creature.

"What in the world?" I murmured.

"*What in the world?*" the creature shrieked. "*What in the world?*"

It writhed and hissed, shrieking and pretty much freaking out while I gaped at it. "What are you?"

Against all better judgment, I slowly made my way forward, staring at this sightless creature with razor-sharp teeth as it spat and hissed, repeating the words that had just come from my mouth.

"What are you doing?" came a grumbling voice.

I whipped around, shining my flashlight on a perturbed-looking Grim.

"What am *I* doing?" I spat. "What are you doing?"

"Nothing. And that's what you'll remember." He strode up with his backpack, opened it and scooped the evil creature inside. With a frown, he turned to me and whispered a few words. "There. Now. In a moment you'll wonder how you got out here, but will just go back to your cabin and will forget all about seeing the *scree*."

I folded my arms (still keeping the light on him) and tapped my foot. "Whatever insanity you think will work on me, it's not doing anything."

He stared at me. I stared at him.

"What is that thing?" I demanded.

He glanced down at his wrist for several seconds and then looked up. "Paige, you should go home."

"I'm not going home until somebody tells me what's going on in this town."

He frowned, checked his watch again. "Have a good night."

He turned to go, and I raced up to him. Ugh. It felt pretty awful being a woman chasing a man. I hadn't done anything so embarrassing for a good twenty years. But I wasn't about to let my ego stop me from finding out the truth.

"What is that thing?"

"Why aren't you forgetting about it? The spell worked. It always does."

"What are you talking about? What spell? What's going on with this town?"

Grim stopped and faced me. "Just go home."

"I am not going home." I raced around Grim and blocked his path. "How did those vines wrap around the creature, or scree, as you called it? And what is a scree?"

He stopped and stared at me. We were almost to the cabin. The outside light was on. Its beam penetrated the trees enough that I could make out the frustration and worry on big bad Grim's face.

"Please," I whispered. "Tell me what's going on. I'm beginning to think that I'm crazy."

Grim peered at me. I mean, he really studied me, like came up close and everything, bringing with him a woodsy scent. "You say vines *wrapped* around the scree?"

"Didn't you see them? They came out of nowhere and stopped it."

Grim rubbed his face. "I didn't do it. You must have."

I threw my head back and laughed. "How exactly would I have done that? Huh? How would I have caused vines to come out of the forest and stop *that*, that *creature* from eating me?"

Grim cocked a brow. "With magic."

I waited a beat, expecting him to say *got you* or *sucka* or something. But he didn't say anything. Instead Grim just stared at me quietly, his big manly manness filling up the forest.

"With magic," I finally said with a heavy dose of sarcasm. "Right. I've got magic. I can shoot lightning from my fingertips. I ride a broom at night and have a black cat as a familiar. Well, world, you got me. You've canceled me but it's all okay because I'm secretly a witch."

"Usually people are excited to hear a thing like this about themselves." He shook his head in annoyance. "But of course you're not."

"What does that mean?"

"It means that it's no surprise you would take a defensive stance on this."

"I am not defensive," I snapped. "I am the most open-minded, non-defensive person that I know."

"Okay. Great. Well, it's been nice chatting with you. Thank you for capturing the scree, but it's your fault it got out in the first place."

"My fault?" But instead of answering, Grim strolled on by me, heading through the bushes toward my cabin. "How is this my fault?"

Sitting on a patch of dirt in front of the cabin was a motorcycle.

Grim opened a box behind the seat and dropped the backpack into it, locking it tight before answering me.

"If you hadn't been playing with my backpack last night, none of this would have happened."

"For your information"—I crossed my arms with dramatic flair—"I didn't play with your backpack. It kept coming over to my side of the bar." I stopped and stared at him, realizing what I was saying. "You're telling me that you weren't pushing it toward me?"

"No."

I pointed at the motorcycle. "You mean *that thing* was inside the whole time, and it was cuddling up to me?"

Grim sighed. "Scree's like witches."

"For the last time, I am not a witch."

"Right." He chuckled. "Keep telling yourself that."

He got on the bike and began to start it up, but I didn't want him to go. I needed answers, and I had the feeling that Grim had them.

I threw out my hand again, gesturing for him to stop. A vine flew out of a tree and wrapped around the front wheel of his bike.

Grim turned and shot me a withering look. "Let me leave."

"I didn't do that," I said quickly. He continued to scowl. "Okay, maybe I did do it. But I don't know how I did it. I don't know anything."

"Well, I suggest you look in a book for that. Or google it. You'll find out a lot that way."

"No, wait." I raced in front of his bike. "Look, I'm sorry. I want to thank you for helping me out this morning. I don't know who you are in the police department, but you gave me a fighting chance in Walter's death. I had nothing to do with it. I swear that to you. But ever since I arrived in town, strange things have been happening. A book fell on me, and the next thing I knew there was a ghost in my house telling me that she came from the book. And ever since then I don't see people as they are, I see trolls and hairy people that might or might not be werewolves, and I also met a vampire. And then that scary monster in your box tried to eat me, and apparently I can cause vines to shoot out from nowhere and attack people."

The more I spoke the more fatigued I became. The words poured out of me, and with them came all the emotions that I'd been feeling the past six months—all the hurt and anger and frustration and even weakness. I'd been punched in the gut ever since going on Dakota's talk show. I didn't know who I was anymore.

"Please," I pleaded with this man who could care less about me, "all I'm asking is for some help. I don't know who I am. I don't know what's going on, and I don't know who to turn to. I realize that you and I got off to a rocky start, and for that I'm sorry. I've been under a lot of stress these past few months, and it doesn't look like that's about to get any better, because now the police think I murdered my ex-husband. But I didn't. Of course not."

Grim shook his head and cursed under his breath. He switched the ignition off and shoved the kickstand down. "Okay," he relented. "I'll tell you what I can."

"Starting with you," I said.

He nodded. "Fine. My name's Grim and I hunt magical creatures for a living."

CHAPTER 11

J nearly burst into laughter, but the hard set of Grim's eyes made me pause. So instead of giggling it up, I said, "I'm sorry, but did you just say that you hunt magical creatures?"

"I did," he growled.

"I didn't realize that you took offense to your own line of work."

"I don't take offense to it." He rose and stepped toward me. With him came an entire cloud of testosterone. "I just didn't want you to make a joke about things you don't understand."

"I wasn't going to make a joke," I said defensively. How did he know I was going to do that? Okay, maybe I wouldn't have joked exactly, but I would possibly have said something sarcastic to break the tension of learning that he hunted magical creatures. Who hunts magical creatures? Apparently big, huge, lumbering lumberjacks who resemble movie stars. "So that's what you do."

He stared into the night air for a long moment. "Let's go inside and discuss this there."

I glanced around. "Why? Some magical creature about to eat us?"

He scowled. "It's always better to be safe rather than sorry. Screes tend to attract other things that are looking for food."

Okay, even if I had wanted to say something sarcastic, at that point there was nothing to even hint at because I was underwater here. I knew about writing and books. I didn't know about magical creatures and such.

I rushed toward the door. "Well, then. What are we waiting for?"

The inside of the cabin looked normal. There wasn't a sign that Snow was hanging about, which was a good thing. I hadn't actually thought about all the specifics, but did ghosts like to watch people shower? Snow and I might have a hard time getting along if she wanted to hang around when I was lounging in my bathrobe.

But anyway, even though I despised Grim mostly, I still offered him some coffee, which he unfortunately took me up on.

"I don't have cream. It all ruined as I was taken down to the police station today. By the way," I said, spooning grounds into a container, "thanks for stopping Cowan from arresting me. Why'd you do that?"

"Because I'd just seen you and you were freaking out."

"I wasn't—" Grim's expression deepened into a scowl. What was it with this guy? Was *scowl* his preferred expression, like pronouns were for some people? "Okay, I was freaking out. I don't understand what's going on."

"That's why I'm going to explain it to you."

"You are?" I pushed the Start button on the coffee maker and turned around, leaning the small of my back against the counter. "Thank you."

He scowled again, and this time I watched his features closely. He was maybe thirty-five, which would have put him around eightish years younger than me. Not that I was counting or anything. Grim had a few fine lines on his forehead, which were nothing compared to the deep craters on mine. I'd Botoxed them but eventually would have to find the money to keep up with my appearance.

The things that I couldn't Botox were the small pockmarks of fat on my arms (I'd given up sleeveless shirts a few years ago), and also the parentheses around my nose and mouth. Those deep lines were the bane of my existence, and pretty Mr. Grim had none of them.

Oh, how beauty was wasted on the young.

He quirked a brow, and I realized that I must've been staring at him. "Oh, sorry. Coffee's done."

With my face burning like someone had doused it in flames, I whipped around and grabbed his cup, taking it over and placing it on the table in front of him.

There was only a small couch in the living area. There wasn't a recliner or even a rocking chair for me to escape to. No, I was forced to sit right beside Grim and all his heady testosterone.

"Thank you," he said after taking a sip of his coffee.

I knew that I sounded surprised by his kind words. "You're welcome."

"I have manners."

"I didn't say that you didn't."

"No, but you looked at me as if I didn't."

I shook my head, unable to lie my way out of that one. "So what do you have to explain?"

"Where do you want me to start?"

"How about at the beginning?"

"The beginning is too far back to go. I don't have my book of Genesis with me."

I playfully slapped his forearm. "Smarty-pants." Realizing that I'd touched Mr. Manly Man, I recoiled and slid my hand between my legs so that it wouldn't be tempted to touch him again. "But start wherever."

"Willow Lake is a magical town. There are more than humans who live here, but I have the feeling that you already know that."

I tugged on my ear. "I'm sorry. Could you say that again?"

"Willow Lake is magical. But most of the time, to humans, that magic is masked. They can't see it. But you did today, didn't you?"

Oh wow. I closed my eyes, not wanting to admit the truth that was staring me in the face. "At first I thought everyone was playing Halloween in the middle of summer."

"You may have thought that for a moment, but you recognized that wasn't the truth. Paige—"

A shiver raced down my spine at the sound of my name on his lips. What was wrong with me?

He continued. "You saw this town as it should be because you're a witch."

I did laugh. "I'm not a witch. Never in my life have I ever tried anything like that."

"What happened? Something about a book?"

I pressed my fingers to my forehead and closed my eyes. "Yes. There's this book in my bedroom. I opened it and it had all these strange stories. I put it away, but not very well. It fell off the shelf and hit me. Next thing I knew, I was talking to a ghost, who doesn't appear to be around right now. Her name's Snow. Anyhow, after that was when I noticed the strange things."

"You hit your head before meeting me, didn't you?"

His question took me by surprise. "Yes. Why?"

"Because that was why the scree kept creeping close to you." He clenched his jaw. "I don't know why I didn't see it before. But I didn't realize you were a witch."

"What? Do witches usually have sparkles shooting from their head or something?" I joked.

"Yes, they do."

Okay then. "Thanks for letting me know."

He sipped his coffee before setting the cup on the table. "So you're saying a book hit you on the head and then you could see magical beings?"

"Pretty much. I know it sounds crazy."

He shook his head. "Not in my world. The book itself must have magical properties. More than likely it awoke something within you, latent abilities."

"I don't have latent abilities."

"Says you."

It was my turn to scoff. "I think that I would know if I did. And I don't."

But hadn't Grandma Taylor been able to see things that my sister and I couldn't? There was one time when Cammi and I had been playing outside and my grandmother had made us go in quickly because she said something was out there, in the pond water. But I couldn't remember any more than that.

Grim slapped his thigh. "Well, that's about all I can tell you. Looks like you're a witch, and now you're living in a magical town."

"Oh, I'm not staying here. I'm only here for the summer." He was starting to get up. "Wait. That's it? You're leaving? I don't know how to do this. I don't know how to be a witch. And there are werewolves and vampires in Willow Lake, in case you hadn't noticed."

He stretched out his broad shoulders that seemed to go on forever. "They don't bite," he told me. "Nothing here's going to hurt you."

"That scree wanted to eat me. So that's not entirely true."

"You have magic. You need to figure out how to defend yourself. Once you do that, you'll be fine."

He headed toward the door. He was going to leave. Just like that. Oh no. Mr. Lumberjack wasn't going to just drop a load of steaming dog poo on my front porch and head out. That wasn't going to happen.

I beat him to the door and blocked it with my body. Listen, when you get old, you stop caring about how desperate your actions might look.

"You can't go. I need someone to teach me."

Grim furrowed his brow. I stared into his eyes and realized that they were silver. Little flecks of brown swam with the silver. "I don't teach beginners."

Which meant that he did teach, or he could. "You're not just a magical creature hunter, are you? In order to see creatures, you must have power as well. Am I right? I know that I'm right."

His jaw flexed in annoyance. Fire shone in his eyes. My heart raced because I might have crossed a teensy-weensy line with this guy.

But it was a risk that needed taking. And as I stared up at him, Grim softened.

Slightly. I wasn't going to leap for joy or anything. But the steely look in his eyes faded slightly. "I don't teach."

"You almost got me killed," I retorted.

"You shouldn't have been outside."

"Oh, is it blame-the-victim time? Do the police know that you let a dangerous creature escape? Do they? If Cowan knew, what would he say?"

Probably something about how great a guy Grim was.

Grim scowled again. "Fine. I'll teach you a little magic. Enough that you can protect yourself. But that's it. Then you need to find someone else to help you. There are plenty of folks in this town who know a thing or two about power. They can give you pointers, if you feel so inclined to learn them."

"Thank you. So. What do we do first?"

He laughed. "I'm not teaching you anything tonight."

I felt a little wounded at that. My heart was tender, and Grim had just squished it a bit. "Why not?"

"Because it's late and I'm tired. And as you've so kindly reminded me, I've got a scree that I need to lock up."

"Where will you put it?"

He ignored my question. "We can start tomorrow." He stared at me. I stared back. "Now. Can you kindly move out of the way so that I can go home?"

Oh. Right. "Sure." I opened the door and followed him out. "How did I do that whole thing with the vines?"

Grim hiked one leg over his bike. "Magic," he replied sarcastically.

"Very funny. I know that. But how?"

"How should I know?" He didn't put a helmet on, I noticed, which did not surprise me in the least. "But if you ever get attacked again, you should use that ability."

I shook my head. "I don't even know how I did it. But maybe you can help me fix that."

He growled in response.

"So that scree"—I glanced at its spot in the box—"why did it want me?"

Grim shot me an amused smile. "Do you really want to know?"

"Yes."

"Because witches are its favorite food."

Oh. Not the answer that I had expected. "Okay. That's gruesome."

"That's not the worst of it." He kicked the engine to life and the motor rumbled. "It's their favorite part of the witch that's the worst of it."

"And what part is that?" Did I really want to know? "What do they like to eat the most?"

"The heart," he said before riding off into the night.

CHAPTER 12

I barely slept that night, and when I did, I dreamed of walking into the cabin's bedroom and seeing Walter dead. Blood seeped down his shirt, and when I moved to walk away, I couldn't. An invisible force kept my feet in place.

Walter's eyes popped open, and he stared at me accusingly. "You wanted me this way, Paige. Well, you got your wish."

He sat up and reached for me. I screamed and the next thing I knew, it was morning. Sunlight streamed through the windows, and I shivered even though there wasn't the slightest chill in the room.

I rose and shuffled into the kitchen to find Snow sitting on the couch reading the paper.

"How are you reading a newspaper?" I asked.

"Oh, it's the *Ghost Times.* They sell it in town." She folded it and placed it in her lap. "I slept there last night so that, you know, we'd have boundaries."

I rolled my eyes. Now I needed boundaries with a spirit. I could see monsters, but apparently boundaries with a local haunting was what I really required.

How lucky I was.

I was just about to make a cup of coffee when a knock came from the door. What? Had Grim woken up early and decided to start our lessons?

I smirked and then realized, what if it was him? Oh no. I grabbed a mirror from my purse and took a quick look. The dark crescents under my eyes screamed for concealer, and my pores were the size of craters.

"Who is it?" I asked.

"Patricia. Your landlady."

"Oh, good." I opened the door. "Would you like some coffee?"

She ignored me and stormed in. "What's this I hear about you murdering your husband in my cabin?"

I belted my robe and glared at her. "*Ex*-husband."

"Ex-husband." She straightened her spine and crossed her arms. Patricia was at least five-ten, and she knew how to use her height to her advantage. "Well? What's going on here?"

"Nothing." I slapped my thigh in frustration. "I didn't kill him."

"That's what they all say."

"They *all*? Who is 'they all'? Do you know more murderers? Is this cabin a cesspool of murder?"

"No, of course not," she said quickly, clearly thrown by my accusation. "But I will not rent to murderers and junkies. Those are the rules."

"Oh, so everyone else is okay?" My gaze darted to Snow, who was back to reading the paper. Apparently ghosts were fine. "You can't just accuse me of murder. Besides, I have it on good authority that you saw Walter here—that you talked to him."

Patricia's apple-sized cheeks turned blush. "I might have seen him."

"I *know* you saw him."

My landlady cocked a brow. "How'd you know that?"

I had promised to keep Estelle's secret. "I heard you," I bluffed.

Her eyes narrowed. I had the feeling that Patricia didn't buy what I was saying, not for one minute, but she wasn't going to challenge me.

"Now," I said. "Do you want to tell me what you were doing talking to Walter, a man who was murdered shortly after?"

"He called me," she said matter-of-factly.

I waited for her to continue. When she didn't, Snow said, "You're gonna have to push her. She doesn't want to say anything that she doesn't have to."

So it seemed. "Why did he call?"

"Your *ex-husband* said that he wanted to surprise you by getting into the cabin before you arrived back. I didn't know he was that *ex*. I thought he was some new man in your life."

"So you just let him in?" What kind of landlady was she? "Weren't you worried about my safety? What if he'd been a murderer?"

She smacked her gums. "Well, that didn't turn out to be the case, now did it?"

She had a point. "Fine. You let him in thinking that he was my boyfriend. What else happened?"

"That was it," she told me. "I don't know anything else."

"Thank you," I said.

"You're welcome." Patricia softened a bit. "I'm sorry for all the trouble. If you need anything, let me know."

I smiled. Patricia was tough on the outside but warm and snuggly on the inside.

She pulled a handkerchief from her back pocket and blew violently into it. Okay, perhaps she wasn't all that warm and snuggly.

"I'll be going," she said, heading toward the door.

"Sure you don't want to stay for coffee?" I asked.

"Nah. I've already had three cups. I don't reckon I need any more."

"No, I suppose not."

She was just through the threshold and I was about to shut the door when she turned to me with a puzzled expression on her face. "One thing I don't get, though."

"What's that?"

"If you weren't meeting your ex-husband here, then why were you on the phone with him?"

My stomach dropped to the ground. "What?"

"The phone. While I was letting him in, he got a call. I assumed it was from you because he was saying 'baby' this and 'baby' that."

"It wasn't me," I assured her.

"Well, okay. Have a good day."

"You too."

As soon as she was gone, I closed the door and pressed my back to it. "Walter was on the phone with someone," I murmured to Snow.

"But you don't know who."

I shook my head. "No, I don't. But I don't remember the police taking his phone yesterday. I didn't see it."

Snow lifted an eyebrow. "You think it's still here?"

"Total possibility." My gaze darted around the room. "Walter was such a scumbag, he might stash his phone before meeting with a woman. You know, in case a second woman would call him."

"Oh, that is dastardly."

"Agreed." I snapped my fingers. "And also, his car wasn't here when I got home. He must've gotten an Uber. There would be a record of it on his phone. We've got to find that cell."

Snow rose. "I'm on it."

It was like Snow and I were suddenly in a mad race to beat each other. Who could find Walter's phone first? I dashed into the bedroom, checking under the bed.

Nothing there.

"Where could he have put it?" I murmured.

On the bookcase? No, nothing there. All right. What about behind something? There wasn't much in the bedroom except for a dresser, a lamp and a rocking chair. The phone wasn't near any of them.

Aha! My panty drawer. I could totally see Walter stuffing his phone in there just to be a weird sicko. But when I pulled the drawer, there was nothing to be found except for my...panties.

Which was how it should have been, I supposed.

With the bedroom checked out, I headed back into the living room. Snow was pouring over the kitchen cabinets, pulling out each individual plate and giving them a good once-over.

"The phone won't be invisible," I told her. "It's not like Walter was a wizard or anything."

Listen to me, talking about wizards. Three days ago I would have thought talk like that was impossible.

"Never hurts to make sure," Snow said.

I ignored her, trying to figure out exactly what Walter would have done with his phone. I never saw any of the policemen carrying it around. So where was it? If I was that low-down, dirty ex-husband of mine, where would I have stashed it?

I had it. I zipped to the bathroom and put my hand behind the toilet and felt something rectangular between the porcelain base and the wall.

"Aha! I've got it!"

And I did. I took the phone back out into the living room.

Snow sailed up to me. "What's that?"

"This is his phone."

"It doesn't look like a phone."

It didn't to her. To Snow's nineties mind, cell phones were big and bulky and looked like landlines. "Um. They've changed a lot."

I pressed the Home button, and the screen flared to life. A patch of numbers appeared, and I put in what I knew to be Walter's last password and pressed Enter. The numbers shuddered before locking tight.

"Crap."

"What is it?" Snow asked with concern.

"It's locked. I can't get in. The only way to gain access is if I put the phone to Walter's face. Great. I'm screwed."

Snow nibbled the edge of her fingernail. "What makes you say that?"

"Well, it's obvious, isn't it? I can't get anywhere near Walter's face. I don't know where he is, and it's not like the police will let me."

"Well," she said slowly, seeming to choose her words carefully, "if nothing has changed in Willow Lake, and I doubt that it has, I know where Walter's body may be."

"You do!" I wanted to kiss her. "Where?"

A slow smile spread across her mischievous face. "Get dressed and I'll show you."

ACCORDING TO SNOW, Willow Lake wasn't big enough to have a proper morgue. But luckily she knew a little bit about how things worked in the town.

I only hoped that much hadn't changed since the late nineties.

"If they're investigating Walter's body, it'll be at Palmer's."

"What's Palmer's?" I glanced over at her in the seat next to me as we drove into town. "Is that a funeral home?"

"No. It's the ice cream shop."

I almost threw up on my steering wheel. It must've been because I hadn't even had coffee yet. With Patricia showing up first thing and then the race to find Walter's phone, I was chugging away well below empty. I was somewhere around empty minus.

"I've got to get some coffee," I murmured as we passed Banshee's Beans, a clear competitor of Witch's Brew. "I don't know if I can get used to all these name changes."

"What do you mean?" Snow asked.

"You know, the fact that this town is full of magical beings. I just don't know."

"Didn't you say that you're a writer? You can always pen it down."

I slowly glanced over at her. My goodness, but she was right. She was so right. Why hadn't I thought of that before. I'd been writing serious paranormal stuff, but this—what was happening to me now was the stuff of comedy genius.

"Snow, I could kiss you."

"I don't think that's possible. I'm a ghost."

I laughed. "Yes, you are."

"Oh, there's Palmer's."

She pointed to a shop with a storefront that had pictures of swirling ice cream cones and colorful striped lollipops. My stomach rumbled. No matter how desperately hungry I was, I would not eat ice cream for breakfast.

Okay, maybe I would.

"Is it open?" I asked.

"Yeah. It's open," she told me. "Palmer's closes late and opens early."

"In this town?"

"Yeah. They serve the vampires."

A shudder worked its way down my spine. "The vampires?"

Snow nodded. "Yep. This is the only place in town to get blood ice cream."

I closed my eyes. "Do I really want to know about that?"

"Don't worry. It's one hundred percent donated blood. But anyway, the vampires say it's amazing, and Palmer's stays open late—you know, because the undead don't need to sleep and all."

My stomach suddenly felt queasy. "Of course. The undead and their sleeping habits get first priority. I completely understand," I said sarcastically.

"Ready?" Snow said before sliding through the door and out onto the street.

"No need to wait for me," I murmured before unbuckling my seat belt and heading out into the early summer morning. "Here goes nothing."

CHAPTER 13

*P*almer's was indeed open as Snow had promised. It was cold inside. Very cold, and I almost wished that I still had my bathrobe on instead of the shorts and light sweater that I was wearing.

I could have also done with a couple hours more sleep while I was at it.

But anyway, I had a name to clear.

A cheery man greeted me. He didn't see Snow; that much was obvious as he totally ignored her. "Good morning, how can I help you?"

He looked to be a teenager with a few red bumps on his face and was tall like a basketball player. He had a nice, lopsided grin, and I spied his name tag. *TOMMY* was chiseled onto it with gold letters.

"Um, good morning," I said, not sure exactly how to start. *Do you have a dead body in the back that I can look at?* That didn't exactly seem to be the way to go on this one. So I settled for the obvious, "I wanted to buy some ice cream."

"Absolutely." He pointed to the case. "I'm assuming you won't want the blood."

"Oh no, I've got all the blood I need," I joked.

Tommy didn't laugh. Instead he started calling out names. "We've got vanilla, chocolate, banana, orange sherbet, rainbow flavor, a heavenly butter pecan that tastes like butterscotch."

My eyebrows lifted at that. "Butterscotch! That sounds—"

A terrible clanging came from the back. Tommy rolled his eyes and waited to speak until it was finished. "Sorry about that. One of the freezers acts up every once in a while. It's a big one, a walk-in."

Oh, which reminded me why I was here. Snow was giving me a big-eyed look as if to hint that I needed to stop thinking about ice cream and do some investigating. Well, little did she know, but my brain needed sugar first. Eating always helped me think.

"So," I said while Tommy scooped up ice cream. "Have you worked here long?"

"Yep, since the fall. I'm saving my money for trade school. Been busting my butt to make extra cash just about any way that I can. Here you go."

He handed me the cone, and I spotted a small blonde hair on his shirt. Tommy wasn't blond. He had dark hair.

I smiled. "You've got something on you there. Must be your girl-friend's."

He glanced down to where I was pointing. "Oops. I don't have a girl-friend. Not sure how that got there."

He plucked the hair off his shirt and let it fall to the floor far, far away from the ice cream chest, I was glad to see.

"Well, enjoy," he told me.

Snow was giving me dark looks at that point. We were here for a reason, and not so that I could stuff my face.

But I did anyway.

The ice cream was heavenly—literally so good. The cream itself tasted like butterscotch, and the pecans added an extra bite to it. It was divine. I would be coming back.

"You like it?" Tommy asked.

"I love it."

He washed off the scoop and splayed his hands across the counter. "Good deal."

"So…about that blood ice cream. I don't see it in the case."

He shook his shaggy head of hair. "No. We keep it in the back. Don't want to scare the humans. The vampires know to ask for it."

I cocked a brow. "You look human. You're not?"

He chuckled. "I'm about as human as you are."

So he was a wizard. Okay. Good to know. "Listen, Tommy. I know that you don't know me, but my name's Paige."

"Oh, I've heard of you. Sorry about what happened with your husband and all."

"*Ex,*" I corrected.

"Yeah." He rubbed the back of his neck sheepishly. "Sorry about that whole thing."

Snow must've gotten tired of me wasting time, because she sailed past the counter. "I'm gonna check the back."

To Tommy I said in a sad, sincere voice, "Look, my ex-husband, I wanted to say goodbye to him. Is he here?"

Tommy grimaced. "Ma'am, I'm not supposed to talk about who we've got in the freezer."

So he was! And wasn't it some sort of health violation to keep dead bodies near where food was prepped?

Tommy must've read my mind (perhaps that was his superpower—I mean, super*natural* power) because he said, "The bodies go in a different freezer."

"I just want to see him one last time. Say goodbye to him."

Tommy nibbled his bottom lip. I just about had him. There was one way to tip him over the edge. I pulled forty dollars from my purse and slapped it on the counter.

"I only need two minutes."

He looked around before sliding the money into his pocket. "Come with me. But anyone asks you, you never saw him."

I gestured crossing my heart. "You got it."

I dumped my ice cream in the trash and followed Tommy to the back freezer. He opened a large steel door and flipped on a light.

"Two minutes," he reminded me.

"Got it. I won't be a second longer."

I stepped inside and shivered. Dang. I really wanted my bathrobe now. And also my cozy slippers. Slippers always made things better.

Snow was already inside. "Here he is."

A morgue table sat squarely inside the silver box of *freezing*. There were shelves in the space, but they were empty of any food. A white sheet draped Walter's body, and I felt a pang of sadness looking down on him.

"Oh, Walter," I murmured. "You stupid fool."

He'd done something to get himself murdered. But what?

I put my fingers on the sheet above the outline of his head and held my breath.

"What are you waiting for?" Snow asked.

"I'm preparing myself."

"For what?"

"To see his face."

"It's not scary. I already took a peek."

My eyes flared in surprise. "You did?"

She shrugged. "Sure. I was in here for a minute by myself."

Well, he couldn't look all that bad if Snow wasn't upset. After all, how much could his appearance have changed in a day? I pulled the sheet down and stared. One thing I would say was that Walter looked at peace.

That gave me some comfort as I pulled his phone from my purse and placed it to his face. The screen immediately unlocked.

"Yes!" I opened the settings and quickly disabled the pass code, and just in time as a knock came from the door.

"Your two minutes are up," Tommy said from outside.

"Coming." Snow and I slipped from the freezer, and I thanked Tommy on my way out. "I appreciate your help. And I keep my promises—this will stay between the two of us."

"Thank you," Tommy said with a smile. "I'd be glad to take your money anytime."

Outside, Snow glanced over my shoulder. "Well? Did you see anything?"

I shook my head. "No. I just unlocked it." There were people out on the street, so I added quietly, "Not here. Let's talk in private."

Snow paused. "Are you talking about them?"

My gaze swept to where she was pointing. "Yes. Those people."

"They're ghosts."

I balked. "They are?"

"Yeah. Look closely."

As I stared unapologetically at the few folks making their way down Main Street, I realized that they were, indeed, specters. Where their feet should have been was...nothing. You'd think that since I'd been staring at Snow's feetless form for a couple of days that I would have been getting used to seeing people without their very bottoms, but I wasn't.

It took me aback every time.

I supposed that said something about me, mainly that I liked to be alive.

"They *are* ghosts," I murmured.

"Told you," she said smugly.

And as I continued to stare, the people, or ghosts, started staring back. Their heads turned as if they knew that I could see them.

Then they started walking toward me.

I had flashbacks of that Michael Jackson video, *Thriller*. When I was a kid, it played on a constant rotation on MTV. I'd been obsessed with it. There's that one moment when Michael Jackson is normal, and then the next second he's a zombie staring at his date with scary googly eyes.

That was how it felt now—like those spirits were staring at me with big creepy eyes.

It took everything I had to resist the urge to run. But maybe I should have, because next thing I knew, they had swooped on me and were shouting at me all at once.

"My family needs to find the treasure I buried," cried a woman dressed from maybe the 1950s.

"I was murdered! Help me find the killer," claimed a man with a massive head wound.

"Someone new has moved into my home. Help me get rid of them," begged a woman.

Fear paralyzed me. I didn't know what to say or do.

Snow stepped forward and pushed the ghosts back. "Stop it. She's my person. Go get your own medium witch."

"But she can see us," argued the 1950s woman.

"I don't care," Snow snapped. "She's busy with her own murder to solve."

Very slowly the ghosts turned away, their heads dragging, their gazes downcast.

"Wow," I said. "Do you think that you were a little harsh?"

Snow scoffed. "You don't have time to fool with those people. You've got to figure out who killed Walter, right? Isn't that the most important thing?"

"Right. To the car."

As soon as we were inside my SUV, I opened Walter's phone. "Maybe he got a text," I said, clicking on the green icon. I scrolled through his messages, but the most recent had been those that he'd sent to me. "Nothing here."

"What about phone calls? Did he get any?" Snow asked.

"Right. Obviously." I laughed. How could I have missed phone calls? I opened that icon and searched. There were several numbers, none of which had names attached to them. I dialed the first one.

"Hello?" came a grouchy female voice.

"Um, hello. This is…the eating chef."

Oh my God. Had I really just called myself *the eating chef?*

"What do you want?" snarled the person.

"Uh, I received an order for you for three dozen crispy-topped cupcakes, and I was wondering where we need to deliver those to."

"Look, I didn't order any cupcakes. And I sure as heck have never heard of them with a crispy topping."

What had I done? I was blowing this. All I needed to find out was who this was. "Well, can you just give me your name and I'll verify the name on the order?"

"This is Patricia."

My landlady. She'd told me that Walter had called in order to have her open up the cabin. That was why her number was on the phone.

"Uh, never mind," I quickly said. "Wrong person."

I hung up before she could question me further. My heart was racing. My palms were sweating. I wasn't cut out for this whole investigating thing.

"Well?" Snow asked.

"It was the landlady. So we can cross her off the list."

"Okay, landlady, clear," Snow said in an authoritative voice. "Who's next on the list?"

"Here's another number. It's from yesterday, too. Yesterday morning. This number didn't go out. It came in. Someone called Walter and it looks like they talked."

"Great. Dial it."

I was just about to when a swish of long brown hair caught my eye. I glanced up in time to see a slim woman in athletic gear slip into a building.

"No," I murmured. "It couldn't be."

Snow's gaze tracked where mine had been. "Couldn't be who?"

I shook my head. "Forget it. Now. Where were we?"

"The number."

"Right." I was about to dial when knuckles rapped on my window. "Ah!" I jumped up and slammed my head against the SUV's ceiling. "Ouch!"

The knocking came again, and when I looked, anger filled me. Grim stood outside my door, glaring at me.

I rolled down the window. "What is it?"

"We had a date."

My heart jumped into my throat. "What?"

"To teach you."

My heart calmed. Lie. It didn't calm. It raced even harder. "I forgot."

He scowled. "Meet me at your cabin in ten minutes and we'll get started."

Okay, well. So much for Walter's phone. It would have to wait because apparently I had a date with Mr. Grim Face.

CHAPTER 14

$\mathcal{M}$r. Grim Face had me shucking it all the way back to the cabin at double speed.

Well, he didn't have me doing it. I supposed that I did that part myself.

When we arrived back at the cabin, he was giving me his most surly face and everything, as if it was completely my fault that he'd tracked me down to Main Street. That had been his choice, if you asked me.

He could have just waited for me to return instead of making such a big deal about it.

But I did want to learn some magic. I mean, I guessed that I wanted to learn. It was almost too much for my brain after what had happened earlier when the ghosts surrounded me.

Did I want to learn magic?

"You don't look excited about this," Grim said.

"I am," I lied. "I mean, I guess that I am. Something weird happened in town."

We were standing outside. Though I'd been tempted to put my bathrobe back on (since it was super cozy), I'd overcome the urge. After all, I didn't want to smell like sleep around Grim because he had the habit of smelling all manly and stuff, like he'd just walked out of the ocean as Zeus's son or something and was ready to tackle a whole bunch of Greek trials that included things like stealing a golden fleece and killing a Minotaur. He would probably be wearing a loincloth the whole time, too.

For some reason I found myself staring at his crotch.

Luckily he didn't notice.

"What happened?" he asked, sounding really annoyed with himself that he was even considering wanting to hear the story.

"Well—" I lifted my gaze from his crotch to his thick biceps. How were they that big? "It happened after I left Palmer's."

"Palmer's? You wanted ice cream this early in the morning?"

"No. Yes. Walter's body is there, and I have his phone. I needed to unlock it so that I could find out who he'd spoken to last. You know, so that I can track down his killer."

Grim stared at me a beat. Then he tossed his head back and laughed. At me.

"What's so funny?"

"You want to find his killer?" He stopped laughing and wiped tears from his eyes. "That's your plan?"

"Do you have a better one? Are you on this investigation?" I was heated up now. "Is this your jurisdiction?"

"I'm more of a consultant."

"What does that even mean? You run around and suggest that they do things like change a lightbulb?"

A dark shadow passed over his face. "Yes. That's exactly what it means."

"No, it doesn't. You're only saying that because I said it." I folded my arms. "Listen, I am grateful to you for helping me out. Can you just forget what I said about Walter and start teaching me magic?"

"You'll wind up getting hurt if you stick your nose in places where it doesn't belong."

"Thank you for the advice." I stared at him, waiting. "Well? Are we going to begin, or am I just going to stand here until the cows come home?"

Grim rolled his eyes. "Let's get started."

I pushed up my sleeves. I was ready to learn this magic stuff. I would tame it just like I tamed the words in my head and turned them into stories.

Or I might not. We would see.

"Okay," he said very grouchily. If he didn't want to teach me, why was he? No one was twisting his arm. "The first thing you need to do is feel your power. Close your eyes and see if you can touch it."

I closed my eyes and focused or concentrated or something on some power that was supposed to be inside me. But all I felt was...hungry. I'd only had a couple of bites of ice cream before dumping it in the garbage, and I still hadn't had my coffee.

"Do you feel it?" he asked.

"Yes."

Why did I lie? I didn't know why. Grim was just so bossy and mean looking. I was afraid that if I said that I couldn't feel my power, that I'd get sent to the principal's office. That would just mean Grim would be even meaner.

"Good," he said in a gravelly voice that was almost like a purr. He really had a very good bedroom voice. It almost made up for what a meanie he was.

Almost.

"Now that you feel your power, see if you can bring it forth and manifest it into a ball in your hands. Be the power. See the magic before you."

"Be the power," I murmured. "Feel the magic."

Maybe if I said it, it would make it happen. I poked and prodded, but only wound up feeling vacant inside except for a rumbling belly.

"Now, do it," he commanded. "Bring your power forth."

I strained and pushed from my gut, trying to bring something out of me—a magic baby.

"Nothing's happening," he said. "Are you even trying?" he added in an accusatory manner.

"Yes, I'm trying. I can feel it. It's so close." Again. Why was I lying? Easy. I wanted to be a good student. I'd always gotten straight As up until high school, when I got my first boyfriend. Then I got a B somewhere in there. When I saw that B, I dumped him. Some things were more important than love. I really should have remembered that before marrying that pervert, Walt—

"Are you focusing?" he growled.

"Yes," I yelped. "One magic baby, coming right up!"

"What?"

"Never mind. Here I go." I tried to tap into something in my gut, but there was nothing there. Nothing. So I made a big show of straining because I didn't want Grim to think of me as a big failure. Because I'd never been a failure until I got canceled and all. "Here it comes," I said, hoping to sound convincing.

"You can't find it, can you?"

I opened my eyes and sighed. "No. Is it that obvious?"

"Yes."

I grimaced. "I'm sorry. I tried. I don't know what happened. Last night I had all this magic coming out of my...somewhere, and now I have nothing."

"It's okay." He placed a hand on my shoulder. Then, seeming to think better of it, Grim dropped said hand to his side as if I had leprosy.

I did not have leprosy.

"What's your magic?" I asked. "You have magic, right? I mean, you can't go around catching magical creatures without magic. I wouldn't think so, at least."

"I have magic," he told me with what looked like amusement sparkling in his silver eyes.

"What can you do?"

He sighed as if he wanted to be somewhere else. Well, he could join the club. I wanted to be someplace where I wasn't a murder suspect and where Walter had never entered into my life and stole ten years of it.

But I digressed.

"Power works differently for different people. Some witches can do what you did and command the trees. Some of us harness lightning."

My jaw dropped. "You can do that, can't you? Harness lightning?"

He ignored my question. "Some use spells and work magic the old-fashioned way. Some people can manipulate time. Some can read minds. Some can disappear."

"You sound like a bunch of superheroes instead of witches and wizards."

"There are different ways of manifesting magic, as I said."

"And what about you? You work spells. Maybe that's what I do, too. Maybe I can work spells."

He opened his palm, and a flame danced in the very center. "This is a simple spell that's in my mind at all times. I conjure the flame. Here. Take it."

"What?" Was he really suggesting that I take fire from him? "You want me to hold it?"

Once again, that amusement was sparking in his eyes. "Yes, hold the flame."

"Will it burn me? I don't know where the nearest doctor is to perform a skin graph. Besides, I have to write sometime today. I'm going to need this hand."

He rolled his eyes. "It won't burn you. I won't let it."

There was something in the way he said that last part that caught my attention. It sounded almost a touch protective.

I must've been imagining it. Grim wasn't a nice person.

I opened my palm (still untrusting as to whether or not I would be burned) and watched as he brought his hand to mine. The side of his palm brushed my flesh, and a shiver shimmied all the way to my tailbone.

I didn't notice the look of focus that Grim had on his face. I also ignored how his hair tickled my palm because he was bent over so far, and I really didn't notice how yummy he smelled.

Yep. I managed to ignore all of that and keep my attention on the flame, which danced across his flesh and wiggled its way onto my palm.

I bit my bottom lip, waiting for the fire to sear my flesh. But all I felt was a coolness as the little flame searched for the spot in the very center of my palm, found its way there and waited.

"Now what do I do?" I whispered, for some reason fearing that if I spoke too loudly the flame would extinguish. "Do I talk to it?"

Grim chuckled. "No. You turn it into magic."

"Okay." I paused. "How do I do that?"

I glanced up at him then and found that he was still hovering very close to me. Grim seemed to realize that as mortal enemies, we weren't supposed to be so close, so he straightened and cleared his throat.

Distance back on, he opened his palm, and another flame lived there. "This can become whatever you want. You can turn it into a ball that can be used in a fight."

"You mean shoot it at someone?" It was a horrible thought. You could kill someone with it. "Hurt them?"

He scowled. "Would you have paused to consider how much the scree would have been hurt last night before he ate you?"

"Good point. Continue."

"Watch carefully." Grim breathed on the flame, and it grew until it was the size of a softball. Then he tossed it up into the air and caught it. "Try that."

I had the feeling that if I blew on my flame, then it would go out, but instead of whining, I just got on with it.

"Before you blow, concentrate on making the magic bigger."

"Okay." Sounded easy enough. "Got it."

I did just as he said, thinking about making the magic bigger. I inhaled, thinking about magic, and exhaled, thinking about magic.

The little flame danced as if it might go out, which made my stomach clench. I could not fail. I didn't want Grim to think I was a total failure. Not that his opinion mattered.

Lucky for me, the flame didn't extinguish. It grew. And kept growing until it was the size of a basketball.

"What did you do?" Grim accused.

"Nothing. What you said."

The ball was so big that it kept inflating past the basketball size until it looked like a beach ball. And it still wasn't done.

"Put it out," Grim commanded.

I shot him a dark look. "I don't know how. I just started working magic yesterday, in case you hadn't realized that."

"Give it to me," he commanded.

"Take it."

He put his hands around it, but the ball kept getting bigger and bigger and it was still in my hands.

"It won't budge," he said. I couldn't see his face, but he was probably scowling. Or brooding. Or something along those lines. "Try it again."

I literally handed the ball over, but instead of plopping into his hands, it shot up into the sky like a firecracker and exploded into a thousand fiery bits that reminded me of lightning bugs.

"Oh, that's pretty," Snow said from the doorway. When had she come outside? "Looks like you're doing well."

"Thanks," I said with a scoff. "But I think that I'm more of a terminal case."

"Who are you talking to?" Grim asked.

I pointed to her. "Snow. She's a ghost. I'm haunted, too. I'm a witch who didn't realize that I was a witch, and I've got a ghost sidekick. What else do you want to know?"

The right side of Grim's mouth curled into a smile. Wow. I hadn't known that he knew how to smile. "Looks like you don't quite have the whole magic thing down."

"You think?" I lifted my hands for emphasis, and a line of fire shot out and hit a pine tree. The branches burst into flames. I wanted to cry. "Ah!"

Grim shook his head. "Don't worry. I've got this."

With a wave of his palm, the flames disappeared. He turned to me and scrubbed a hand down his cheek. "I'm hungry. What do you say we get a bite to eat?"

"With you?" I asked skeptically.

He laughed. "Do you see anybody else here?"

I pointed to Snow.

"She doesn't count," he corrected.

"Okay," I said. "Let's do lunch."

"Good. I know the perfect place."

CHAPTER 15

$\mathcal{A}$ ll that fire must've burned away a little of Grim's brain or something. I couldn't figure out why else he would have asked me to lunch. It wasn't like we were friends.

We were definitely not friends.

But even though we weren't friends, I still hopped on the back of his motorcycle (while Snow catcalled) and held on to his very hard-like-a-tree stomach as we zipped down along the lake until we reached a small cafe.

"You're not a vegetarian, are you?" he asked after we'd gotten off the bike.

I couldn't resist screwing with him. "Yes, I am. Actually I only eat grass and daffodils. Do you think they serve that? Otherwise it's a no-go for me."

He rolled his eyes. "Smarty."

"Just keeping up with you."

He held the door open for me (I still didn't know why) and we slipped inside. We took a booth in back, and a very pale waitress with long ebony hair slinked up.

"The usual, Grim?" she asked.

"You got it, Sally," he told her.

Sally smiled at me, but it wasn't friendly. It was more like a cautiously-checking-me-out kind of look like she was jealous that I was sitting with Grim. Well, she had nothing to worry about because I wasn't interested in all his manliness. She didn't realize it, but apparently I was only good at attracting perverts.

"And for you?" Sally asked me.

I'd skimmed the menu, but nothing had popped out. "Whatever he's having."

Grim cocked a surprised brow. "You sure?"

"Is it raw squid or something?"

"No."

"Then I'll take it."

"Sure thing." Sally took the menus. "Be right back."

When she was gone, Grim studied me. "So you shot a fireball into the air and then you set a tree on fire."

I winced. "I'm sorry. It was an accident. Do you think the tree will die? I can have it replanted." With money that I pulled out of my butt. "Or I'll do something else."

"The tree will be fine." He was quiet for a moment. "Tell me about the magic."

Was that a trick question? "I don't know any more than you."

Sally brought us each a water, and I sipped it gratefully. Working all that magic had made me parched.

"So the thing about the fire I gave you," Grim explained, "is that it was an illusion. What you did was summon actual fire. That's completely different. And I've never seen anyone do that right off the bat."

"Oh, okay. Well, let's chalk it up to beginner's luck."

"I don't think so."

"I think so," I said.

He made a little noise in his throat that sounded like a reprimand. "What happened to your ex-husband? I know that he was murdered, but why? Do you think?"

"Because he was a horrible person?" I said with a scoff.

"Was he?"

"Yes, he was. I'm not going to go into it, but trust me, the world is better off without him. Not that I did anything to him." I made a chopping motion with my hand and realized that could have been seen as

89

being violent. "At one point I loved him, but the divorce was messy. But I tell you, there were things that Cowan missed when the police did their investigation."

Grim quirked a brow. "What do you think they missed?"

"A butt print."

He watched me with a quizzical expression. "A butt print?"

"Yes, from a small butt. I found it on the counter. I hadn't sat there, and I'm trying to track down whose print it is."

He nodded, seeming to really be jiving with my whole butt-print idea. I knew that I was on to something! "And how will you do that? Measure people's bottoms?"

"By sight," I confirmed. "Obviously I can't pull out a measuring tape when I talk to someone and ask if they'd please turn around."

Or could I?

"So you think that's a solid clue."

"Snow showed it to me."

He quirked a brow. "Snow?"

"The ghost," I reminded him. "You know, the one who came out of the book."

"Right." Sally brought our food (she served Grim first) and my mouth dropped. "Something wrong?" Grim asked, sounding amused.

"Nope, nothing's wrong," I told him. I should have looked at the menu. I never should have ordered what he was having because Grim was eating three fried eggs, at least twelve pancakes sitting in a pond of golden amber syrup, and two huge chunks of Polish sausage.

I'd never be able to eat all of that. I'd only make a small dent in it. And all those carbs in the pancakes. I'd weigh three extra pounds by tomorrow if I consumed it all. But perhaps the extra layer of fat would keep me alive after all my money was gone.

"Can I get you anything?" Sally asked.

Another stomach? "Nope. Everything looks great."

As soon as she was gone, Grim said, "You don't have to eat all of that."

"Thank goodness. I don't think I can anyway."

"I'll eat what you don't."

"Are you sure?" I asked. "This is a lot of food."

He winked. *Winked!* "I can handle it. But tell me about the book."

"Oh, right. It was by some Heronomous Bosch guy."

"That was a famous painter," Grim told me.

"Well, the name was something like that, and I happened to read Snow's story."

"She had a story?"

He took a bite of pancake, so I felt obligated to nibble a little bit. They were perfect. The edges were crispy and wonderful, and the cake itself was moist and spongy.

"This is heaven," I moaned.

"They cook them in bacon fat, that's why."

"I'm sure I'll die of a heart attack as soon as I get home," I complained.

He chuckled. "I doubt it would be that soon. But no, you can't eat this stuff every day."

"Unless I'm young like you."

"You're young," Grim said. "You can't be any older than me. I'm thirty-five."

I knew it! I was so good at guessing ages. But I had lied about mine the other night when I said thirty-nine. Well, it wasn't as if anything serious was going to happen between me and Mr. Grumpy. So I didn't care.

We looked at each other appraisingly, as if we both admired the other for still being in their thirties. And Grim kept looking at me. Was there something in my hair? I hadn't even brushed it that morning. I'd only run my fingers through it because sometimes it looked better without a good brushing.

So why was he staring at me?

"The book," I said, clearing my throat so that he'd stop staring at whatever hideous zit he'd found on my face.

"The book," Grim agreed. "You were saying something about Snow's story?"

"Right. I read a page about a woman who disappeared. Next thing I knew, the book fell on my head and knocked me out."

"Must've been some heavy book."

"I guess. It didn't look that big. But when I came to, Snow was standing over me explaining that she'd been inside the pages and that I'd let her out. Well, of course seeing a ghost scared me, so I hightailed it out of there. That was when I met you and Ferguson." I leaned forward. "Did you know that he wears false legs?"

"He's a leprechaun."

I nearly spat out a pancake. "What?"

Grim nodded. "Just about everyone in Willow Lake is something."

"But I've been here before," I argued. "Walter and I used to vacation here when we were first married. It wasn't like that then."

"Oh, how little yea know," he said, amused. "Humans can't see the magical things like werewolves, vampires, shape-shifters. There's a spell on the town to stop them from witnessing it. So they see mist or smoke, or even nothing."

"Like I used to," I said, chewing on a bite of sausage. "But do you think it's really possible that I somehow managed to gain powers so quickly from being hit in the head with a book?"

He considered that. "So you're saying that this book housed just Snow?"

"Oh no. There were lots of other pictures."

He leaned in. "Of what?"

The steely tone to his words caught me off guard. I didn't want to get this wrong. It felt like I was back in school being quizzed. I had been very competitive in those days.

"Let me see. I think there were creatures in there, too. A monster or two. Yes, definitely a monster. I remember one squid-looking thing with eyeballs all over its body."

The sound of cutlery clattering made me look up. Grim had dropped his fork. "An *aghash*?"

I shrugged. "I don't know what it was called, but it had lots of eyes. Like I said, there were other things in there, too."

Grim sat back and studied me for. A. Very. Long. Time. "So this book, is it still at the cabin?"

"It should be. I didn't move or take it. Just placed it back on the shelf."

He grabbed his jacket and rose. "Let's go."

Had I missed a memo? "Where to?"

"The cabin. We need to get that book locked away before anyone else gets ahold of it."

"Why?"

"Not here." He threw down a few bills. I moved to open my purse and he said, "On me. You can get the next one."

As if. He didn't know it, but I was scrimping. There wouldn't be a next one.

As soon as we were outside, Grim turned to me. "That book you told me about, I've heard of it but didn't believe that it existed."

"Okay." I had no idea what else to say. "It does."

"If a book like that got into the wrong hands, that person could wreak all kinds of damage on Willow Lake and other towns and cities."

Why would someone do that? "I suppose they could."

He frowned. "There are bad people in the world. You know that, right? One just killed your husband."

"*Ex*-husband." Why did everyone keep calling Walter my husband?

"Right." He got on his bike and I followed suit. His stomach wasn't even bulging, and he'd eaten most of his food. I would have noticed. What was he made of? Steel? "In my years chasing down magical creatures, if there's one thing I've learned, it's that when witches and wizards get control of such an animal, it's never used for good. It's always used to harm or even kill others. So like I said, if that book got into the wrong hands, all kinds of evil could be unleashed on the world."

"Sounds like a horror movie."

"It is. Hang on tight," he said over his shoulder. The sunlight jumped off his straight jawline.

Not that I noticed.

Within minutes we were on the road that wrapped around Willow Lake. The water was beautiful. The sun bounced from the small crests, making the lake shimmer. Boats motored up and down the lake. Some pulled skiers; others carried fisherman quietly trolling the shores.

This was why I had come here, to be refueled by nature. Which reminded me. I had to get to writing. But first, the book.

We arrived at the cabin within minutes. "I'll show you where it is," I said, leading Grim inside.

He looked strange inside the small space, as if the cabin wasn't large enough to contain his manly energy.

I led him to the bedroom. "It's in here."

He followed me and we started scanning the shelves. I knew that I had placed the book on the very top one.

"It should be there." I pointed to a spot. "But it's not."

"Let's search them all."

We scanned each and every book, looking for what felt like an hour before Grim finally said, "It's not here."

I sucked air as I realized, "It's been stolen."

CHAPTER 16

"The only people other than the police who've been inside the house since I found the book is Walter—Patricia. But she could've taken the book any time before," I told Grim.

"You're forgetting one person," he said darkly.

"The butt-print owner," I realized.

He shot me a withering look, and I decided to keep the butt print to myself.

"We have to find that book," he said grudgingly. "I'll talk to Cowan and see what leads he has."

Grim was about to walk out of the cabin when I remembered something. "I have Walter's phone. The police didn't find it when they were here because my sorry ex had hidden it behind the toilet."

"Why would he do that?"

I rolled my eyes. "Because that's how Walter was. But I was going through his phone calls and texts when you tracked me downtown this morning."

He held out his hand. "Give it to me. I'll take it to the police."

"No."

Impatiently he wiggled his fingers. "I'm not joking."

"Neither am I. The police think I did this. Why would they look at any other suspects when they've got an ex-wife telling her ex-husband that she would kill him?"

"Did you do that?" he whispered.

"I may or may not have done so in the heat of an argument when Walter was trying to get more money out of me." I laughed maniacally. "Little did he know, but he'd already taken it all."

Grim was silent and I had the idea that I'd just given him way too much information. "I'm sorry," he said, surprising me.

"It's okay. But you see that if you give them the phone, then what will they do with it? Find out the Walter had texted me asking for money? Which he had. It'll just be another nail in the coffin of their case against me. So no. I keep it."

He folded his arms. "Okay. You keep it."

Wait. Had that just been so easy? "You mean that?"

"Sure. You keep the phone, but I want to hear the messages."

I squinted at him skeptically. "You promise?"

He laughed. "Yes, I promise. I'm not going to snatch it from your hand and run out the door."

"All right," I said, still unsure if I could trust him. I pulled the phone from my pocket and scrolled through the past calls. Grim moved to stand beside me. He was so close I could feel heat floating from his body and into mine. He was like a furnace. I liked it. Kind of. "This number is Patricia's, the landlady. I spoke to her this morning. She told me that Walter had called her wanting to be let into the cabin, to surprise me, she had thought."

"But you don't think so."

I shrugged. "I don't know. If he'd come to surprise me, how did he end up dead? It doesn't make sense."

"Okay. And the other numbers?"

"I don't recognize them."

"Let me dial one."

My heart raced as I handed the phone to Grim. He clicked on the number and waited as it rang. A moment later he hung up. "It goes to a voice-mail box that's full. There's no message telling me who the number belongs to."

"Hmm." I took the phone back. "The other numbers are from days ago, from before he ever arrived here." I hit the button for voice mail and saw that Walter had received a message just yesterday, before he'd been killed. "What's this?"

I pressed the button and hit Speaker so that Grim and I could both hear, but all that played was some weird clanging. It seemed vaguely familiar, but I couldn't place it. No voice or anything came on the line.

"Huh. That seems like a dead end."

Grim was a little more astute. "Whoever it was waited to see if Walter would pick up. When he didn't, they hung up."

"And the number?"

"Unknown," Grim said. "Which doesn't help us at all."

"So let me see—we've got nothing to go on except a butt print."

"I think you're putting too much stock in the posterior of a person."

"I'm right on this."

He didn't say anything, which basically suggested that I wasn't right. Well, I would show him.

Maybe.

"I'll keep trying the other number," I said, "the one that went to voice mail."

Grim nodded. "I get the feeling that the person who killed your ex-husband may not have been here for him."

"The book," I said. "So you think that they knew about it, came here looking for it, found him, convinced Walter to climb into my bed and then stabbed him with a kitchen knife?"

He didn't look so sure at that. "Maybe they surprised Walter and he was really waiting for you. Before he had a chance to move, they pushed him down and killed him."

I shook my head. "They would've had to know he was here. Otherwise they wouldn't have had a knife, and Walter's vehicle wasn't here. He probably got an Uber."

"Do you see an Uber app on his phone?" Grim asked.

I quickly scanned the contents and my heart sank. "No, I don't."

"Then the killer brought him here on some pretense, which was why you found him in bed. But what they wanted was the book, plain and simple. So they killed him, took the book and left the body to make it look like you did it."

Impressive. I cocked a brow at Grim. "You talk like you've done this before."

He smirked. "I have. Like I said, I consult the police."

"So you used to be an officer."

His expression darkened. "Let me know if you find anything. Meanwhile I'll be asking around, see who may know anything."

He wasn't leaving that easily. "Wait a minute. That's it? I'm on my own on this? No way."

He sighed and stared up at the ceiling for a moment as if to ask God, *Why me?* Then he placed his hands on his hips and shifted his weight. "Exactly what do you have in mind here?"

"I thought that we could work together."

"I work alone."

"Well, so do I," I said just as grimly as he had. "I'm an author. That's what I'm used to—solo ono." Whatever that meant. "But in this, we need to partner up. You know people that I don't. You also know magic."

"You could know it."

"Can we please just not go there right now?" I fumed. "If I don't find the killer, the cops are going to arrest me. I need your help as much as I don't want to admit it. And I think you might need mine."

His brow lifted like ten feet. "Really? How do I need you?"

Had to think of something fast. "Well, you need me because... because...I know what the book looks like."

"What's it look like?"

"I'm not telling." Realizing that I was being childish, I added, "Please. Just this once, and you could use me as a front to help you."

"How so?"

"Tell people that I'm paying you to unravel this mystery."

"I don't work for anyone," he growled. "Besides, you just said that you were broke."

"But they don't know that. Please." I hated to beg, but that was what I'd become—a broken, begging author.

He exhaled a gust of air. "Fine. I'll work with you." I started to clap, but he cut it short with, "But you go by my lead. If I tell you that you can't do something, you listen. No questions asked."

"Got it. No questions." I gave him a genuine smile. "Thank you."

Without another word, he stalked from the cabin and left, leaving me wondering exactly how, if we were working together, I would be communicating with him at all.

~

Right after Grim left, I got a text from Madeleine asking how the writing was going. Since I'd put off sitting down at my computer for long enough, I decided to start hashing out a story about a fake circus psychic (the psychic part was fake, not the circus) who gave a false reading to a witch, who then cursed her to always see the truth. I was loving it. The words were flowing quick and easy, and my heroine, a single mother who'd only lied about being fake because she needed money to raise her kid, was really blossoming as I typed.

The only problem was, I didn't know if Madeleine was going to love or hate my story. It was completely unlike my ghost books. But after half a day of plugging in words, I was committed. I would not stop writing this story now, not even if Madeleine told me that it would never sell. I didn't care. I'd take up waitressing in order to make ends meet.

Could I even take an order?

Psha. Of course I could. How hard could it be to marry ketchup bottles and serve drinks?

When I finally looked up from the computer, the sun was setting fast and I realized that I was getting hungry. There wasn't much to eat in the house, which meant that I'd have to hunt up something in town.

Snow was nowhere to be seen, and since I didn't know where she'd gone off to, I debated whether or not to leave her a note telling her.

Did ghosts read notes?

Deciding it was better to be polite than not, I penned a quick note telling her that I'd gone out to eat, and then I left it on the counter.

Hmm. Why would Snow look at a counter when she was dead? Thinking better of my decision, I picked up the piece of paper and deposited it on the coffee table. After all, I'd spotted Snow over in that area reading the *Ghost Times* or whatever that paper had been called.

Satisfied with my decision, I grabbed my purse and opened the door.

Then I screamed.

A short, fat lady stood in the entranceway holding what looked like a casserole dish.

"Heard you all alone," Estelle said, "so I made you a chicken casserole."

I frowned. "You heard me all alone?"

She smiled widely. "I got that good hearing, you know."

Right. When people first thought up the *shot heard around the world,* I don't think they realized that someone like Estelle could have literally heard it.

"Come on in," I said. "I was just about to head out, but I'd prefer some company. Did you bring your cards?"

She handed me the dish and said with a twinkle in her eye, "Did I bring the cards? What do you take me for, a card shark?"

Well, she was old and obviously bored if her only entertainment was listening to how quiet my cabin was from half a mile away, so...yes, I did think she had nothing better to do than to be a card shark.

I put my purse away and took two plates from the cabinet. "What would you like to drink?"

"You got any wine?"

Estelle did not seem to be the type who drank, but you never knew about someone, did you? "I may have a bottle of white wine in the fridge."

Estelle sat at the tiny dining table and smiled. "Crack her open and let's get to know one another."

Her wish was my command.

CHAPTER 17

"That was before Cowan was put in charge," Estelle said. "The day that he arrived, the first thing he did was to declare that no one was allowed to wear rubber boots ever again."

I laughed. "Because of the sloshing sound?"

"Because everyone in town was laughing at the police and calling them 'duck feet.'"

It may have been the wine (it probably was), but Estelle was the funniest person I'd met this whole time. She was hands down more charming than that sour Grim and had more sense than Cowan, who clearly had a penchant for getting sidetracked and offering way too much information about nothing.

"All because of the last sheriff, who made sure their shoes squeaked so that people knew when the police were approaching?" I said, wiping tears from my eyes.

"Exactly." Estelle laughed, and as her cackling died down, she stared at her empty plate of casserole and the half glass of wine. "Bottom's up," she said before tossing the rest of the liquid down her throat.

I lifted the bottle and moved it in tantalizing circles. "Want more?"

"No, one's enough for me. I'm too old to hold my liquor."

I set the bottle down. "I completely understand."

Our conversation died and Estelle said, "So how long have you been a witch?"

The mouthful of wine that had been in my mouth suddenly ejected onto my empty plate. "Oh, sorry. You took me by surprise. A witch? How did you know?"

"Because you have sparkles coming from your head."

"Grim said that I didn't."

"Grim can't see them because he's much too busy to look. Thinks he's got more important things to do."

I scoffed. "Tell me about it. He's the most frustrating person I've ever met. Tried to teach me magic and that didn't go well, so he took me out to lunch. I don't know whatever for because then he got mad because this magical book hit my head and turned me into a witch, and now the book's gone and I'm talking to ghosts and can see werewolves." I leaned in conspiratorially. It might have been a bit of the wine talking when I added, "Did you know that werewolves are really, really furry people?"

Estelle clapped her hands. "Yep, you're a witch all right. So. How'd Grim teach you magic?"

Out of all of that, Estelle was more interested in the lessons than anything else? She wasn't even interested in the book? Okay, then.

"Well, he had me take some fire from his hands and make it bigger, but it kept growing and then I launched a flame at a pine tree and nearly killed it. I'm really unteachable."

"Nonsense. Grim just expects to bulldoze into a situation and make it work, because that's how he thinks." Estelle placed her hands in her lap. "There's nothing wrong with that. It serves him well when he's hunting down monsters and critters that aim to hurt us—and trust me, there are lots of them. Why just this week he tracked down a scree that was killing livestock outside of town."

"You mean the scree that almost killed me?"

"Woo, girl, you must have a lot of witch juice in you for a scree to want your heart."

"Please don't remind me." I rubbed my forehead. When was I going to wake up from this nightmare? "But anyway, the creatures are often here? Outside of Willow Lake?"

"Magical creatures are attracted to magical people. We need folks like Grim to keep us safe."

Huh. And I needed him to help me find a killer, but it didn't appear that he would be calling me anytime soon about that.

"But anyway," Estelle said with a big smile on her face, "let's get you learning magic."

"What? Why?"

She stared at me blankly. "Because you're a witch."

"An accidental one."

"And an accidental medium at that, too. Not every witch can see spirits. Which means that whatever happened to you—a book hit you?"

"Conked me right on the head," I confirmed, pouring myself another finger of wine. "I'd never had any kind of power before that. I wish that I could just give it back. But the book's gone."

She clasped her hands. "Now. Time to start."

"Do we have to?"

She got a stern look on her face—brows knitted, lips pursed, the sort of expression that suggested you were a hair away from getting a spanking.

"Yes, you have to," Estelle snapped. "Unless you want to be a sitting duck for every evil creature that comes around, you must learn magic. At the very least, to defend yourself."

I exhaled a gusty sigh and let my glass thunk onto the table. "All right. What do we do first?"

"First we figure out what kind of witch you are."

"Okay. How do we do that?"

"When I was back at the academy, we tested what you were more comfortable with. We started with elements."

I lifted my hand to stop her right there. "Whoa. You went to an academy? I knew Hogwarts was real!"

She laughed. "Not Hogwarts—the Southern Magical Academy. It's down in South Alabama, where all the best witches are."

I lifted a brow. "Fascinating."

"Yes. But anyway, let's start with the basics." Estelle clapped her hands, and a piece of ice appeared in her palm. "Since you had such a hard time with fire, let's try ice first." She dropped it into my palm, and it took everything that I had not to wince in pain as it chilled my flesh. "We're going to turn this into powdery snow."

That sounded like I needed one of those shave ice machines, a little elbow grease and a much larger piece of ice.

"All you need to do," Estelle told me, "is think of trimming it and changing it. If ice is your element, it should work with you easily. The ice should want to help you."

"Like it's my friend?" I couldn't help but to sound sarcastic. This was lunacy.

"Like you're dancing partners," she cooed—actually cooed. "Just focus on the ice and let it work."

So I did as she said, focusing and also thinking about when the last time was that I got my nails done because they were beginning to grow out.

"Are you concentrating?"

"Of course," I lied, trying to refocus myself. "Here we go. Snow."

I stared at the ice, and the ice stared back at me. But then I began to feel a swirl in my belly as if a small dragon was uncoiling from a deep sleep.

Don't ask me why I pictured a dragon in my belly, but the image worked.

It seemed to uncoil the more I focused on it, and a little bit of hope rose in my throat. The ice, in fact, was started to shake. All I had to do was turn it to snow and I'd know what I was then—an ice witch.

Oh, that didn't actually sound good, did it? It sounded one letter away from being a nasty slur.

The ice rumbled like it was about to turn; then it zipped out of my hand and crashed out the window, smashing the glass in its wake.

My jaw dropped as tears welled in my eyes.

"Well, you're not an ice witch," Estelle said cheerfully.

"How can you sound so happy? I just broke a window."

She shrugged and waved her hand. Next thing I knew, an outside vine was dropping the broken shards back into place.

"Is that vegetation fixing the window?" I asked in disbelief.

She winked at me. "Vegetation is my domain. So yes, it is mending it. You can do just about anything with magic, never forget that. Now, what element is next? Oh, I know. Let's try lightning."

A vision of the house burning filled my head. "How about we go outside?"

"Sure thing," she said, sounding chipper.

We went outside and Estelle somehow found a tiny lightning bolt to work with, but it went much the same way as the ice had. I had absolutely no power over it. I couldn't make the lightning do anything except destroy a large rock sitting near us, and that had been on accident.

I was only glad that the bolt hadn't struck either one of us.

Then I remembered something. "The other night when the scree attacked me, vines came to save me."

"Well that's it, then," Estelle said happily. "You have vegetation powers. Why didn't you tell me sooner?"

"I guess I didn't think about it."

"Let's get you going, then." Estelle magicked up a little flower and placed it in my hands. "Make it grow."

I aimed my attention at the flower, putting all my inner drive into it. After all, I was once a best-selling author. That sort of title didn't come by sitting on my rump and waiting for life to take *me* by the horns. No way. I had roped that bull and forced it to bend to my will.

I concentrated super hard—so hard that sweat sprouted on my brow. But nothing happened.

I supposed that was better than it exploding in my face.

But when one petal didn't even shiver, I knew that I must've been doing something wrong. I was working so hard, focusing so intently that maybe a change of tactics would work.

I don't know how the idea popped into my mind. God must've planted it there, but I puckered up my lips and blew. I thought of that dragon in my belly, and I blew it into the flower.

And what do you know, but the petals shuddered and grew.

As I gave it more air, the flower drank up the magic and it bloomed until sitting in my hand was a robust purple flower that I sort of wanted to make into a corsage and display on my wrist proudly for everyone to see.

My jaw dropped as I looked at Estelle and exclaimed, "I did it! I really did it! I made a flower grow."

She beamed at me. "My dear, I would say that we've discovered your witchy talent. You are a vegetation witch. Your power lies in the plants and trees. You are connected to the earth in a way that most are not. Congratulations."

I smiled. "Great. This calls for more wine."

CHAPTER 18

*B*ut the next day I couldn't repeat the magic. Estelle and I had worked for another hour on making vines plump and getting tree branches to sprout leaves, yet the next day I was a total failure.

"Just wait, Snow. Let me show you. I can do this."

She yawned as if she was bored. A ghost, bored! "Take your time."

I had the same sort of flower in my hand that Estelle had given me. I huffed and puffed, but it didn't move. "I swear that I did this last night. It grew."

She gazed over at the empty wine bottle. "Are you sure?"

"Yes, I'm sure." I grabbed the bottle and tossed it in the trash. "Let me give it one more shot."

But no matter how much I blew, the flower did nothing. What was I doing wrong?

"You know what you need?" she said. "Retail therapy. That's what you need."

My phone rang and the caller ID said that it was the police department calling. I cringed and let it go to voice mail. "No, what I need is to find Walter's killer." I opened my fridge, looking for creamer for my coffee, and remembered that I'd had to toss it in the garbage. "And I also need creamer. Looks like I'll be doing that first."

"I'll come with you," she said.

We hopped into my SUV. As soon as I closed the doors, my phone pinged that I had a voice-mail message. My stomach twisted. I *wanted* to hear what Cowan had to say and I didn't. I could just hear him. *We need you to come down to the station. You remember where that is, right? Head into downtown and take a left at the grocery store. Take a right two blocks after that. If you've reached the Stop and Save, you've gone too far.*

No. I didn't want to listen. He'd just have to call me back. If he asked why I didn't return the first call, I'd claim phone trouble and say I hadn't received the message.

There. Problem solved.

Snow and I hit the grocery store, and that time I did much better at not staring at the werewolves. I even pretended not to notice how sharp the vampire checkout girl's teeth were.

"Did you see her fangs?" Snow whispered when we left.

"It's not polite to talk about other people."

"When I was alive," Snow murmured, "there were a lot more vampires and werewolves here."

I stopped loading groceries and stared at her. "You were a witch?"

She laughed. "Of course." Then she stopped and thought. "That might have something to do with why I was trapped in the book."

Before I had a chance to reply, a blonde head caught my attention. The golden tendrils were pulled back into quite a snatch of a ponytail. She wore a black and pink fashionable tracksuit and bright white sneakers that looked more for wearing out than exercising in.

"Quick, hide," I said to Snow, which was ridiculous because no one could see her except for me.

Snow glanced around. "Why are we hiding?"

"Um, we're not."

The blonde head was coming toward me, and I worked hard to bury my nose in the rear of my SUV while I pretended to be rooting around my groceries.

When I assumed it was safe to come up, I leaned back and felt triumphant that I was not seen.

But there she stood, right in front of me. Melissa's eyes widened and she looked about ready to drop her purse and run. I felt the same but instead forced a bright smile.

"Melissa, so good to see you."

"Um, you too, Paige. How are you?" she asked, keeping at least ten feet between us.

"Great. How's the old neighborhood?"

"You know, same old same old."

Melissa shifted her weight from side to side as if trying to figure out how to sprint off and end our conversation.

I kind of wished she had.

"I heard what happened to you, about the canceling and all," she told me, sincerity in her voice. "It's a shame what they're doing to people out there. It's a terrible mob mentality."

"It is."

But for once I realized that I hadn't woken up thinking about being canceled. I'd had other, more pressing matters to attend to. There were things more important than being canceled. There was another world beyond that.

"How are you dealing with it?" Melissa asked.

"It's not that bad," I told her. "It's not that great. I don't tweet my name or anything, not unless I want to feel destroyed. But being out here at the lake helps. So, what are you doing here?"

She shrugged. "We come out every once in a while. Rent a cabin. I'm just in to do some shopping."

"Oh? I didn't realize that you vacationed here. All the years of being neighbors, you didn't mention it."

Melissa was one of those housewives who had all the time in the world to fix herself salads and exercise every day. Her skin was creamy and her complexion clear.

She smiled tightly. For some reason I'd put her on edge. "Well, Paige, it wasn't as if we were close neighbors. We didn't become close until Walter fell out of that tree."

And there it was—the elephant in the room thrown right in and charged with dynamite, exploding in my face.

"This is the woman that Walter peeped on?" Snow said, flabbergasted.

"Melissa, I'm sorry about that," I said sincerely. Wait. Melissa had *known* that Walter was peeping on her? If so, why hadn't she told the police?

My eyes narrowed as if I were some seasoned detective too smart for his own britches. But it was Melissa who spoke. "Well, I'm just glad that everything is going okay for you. Is Walter doing all right?"

"Um, well, he's not doing so good. He, um, was found dead."

"Oh no," Melissa said, but coldly, without any sympathy. "Heart attack?"

"Yes, the kind caused by a knife through the heart," Snow said.

"Not exactly," I told Melissa. "It was intentional. Someone killed him."

"That's terrible that something like that would happen here, in Willow Lake. This is such a nice community."

My brain did some sort of little flicker, like a lightbulb threatening to go out. "I didn't say that he was killed here."

Melissa smiled but her facial features didn't move. Oh, she'd had some Botox. No one in their thirties had a forehead that tight. "You must have mentioned it."

"No, I didn't. I never said that Walter was here."

Melissa cleared her throat nervously. "Oh, would you look at the time? I have somewhere to be. Must get going. Great seeing you, Paige. I wish you all the best. I mean that."

And then she just walked off as if we'd never been neighbors and my husband hadn't tried to peep on her.

The nerve.

But as I watched her tiny rear end swish this way and that as she jogged down the street to get as far away from me as she could, an idea formed.

I pulled my phone out and hit one of the numbers that had called Walter, the one with the filled-up voice mail.

And heard it ring.

Melissa paused to pull it from her purse. Even though her face wasn't turned toward me, I could practically see her frowning at the screen, trying to figure out who was calling her.

She finally answered the call. "Hello?"

My stomach whirled with a thousand butterflies. "Exactly why did my ex and now *dead* husband receive a phone call from you before he was murdered?"

She turned around to face me and killed the call. "All right. You caught me. I spoke to your husband before he died. That's how I knew he was here. But I didn't murder him."

"Perhaps you should tell me the whole story."

She nodded. "Let's grab some coffee, and I'll do just that."

WE WENT to Witch's Brew, and there, I finally understood what Grim and Estelle had been talking about when it came to the sparkles above witch's heads.

The baristas inside, two women who looked like sisters, didn't have green skin and wear pointy hats (though they did wear all black and Doc Martens on their feet). But their heads had little fireworks that shot up every couple of minutes or so.

It was wild.

What was also wild was that in one corner of the cafe sat a group of ghosts all reading the local paper and talking.

"I'll catch up to you," Snow told me as she trailed off to the table.

I caught enough of their exchange to see them look up when Snow appeared and for the ghosts to glance over at me. It seemed that one of them wanted to come over, but Snow blocked their path. He sat again and did…ghostly things, whatever that was.

Melissa peered into her cup of coffee. "I'm sorry that I lied to you."

My stomach rumbled. "Want some food?"

"No. This is my lunch."

"A cappuccino?" I said, startled.

"The milk has enough calories to get me to dinner."

No wonder she had a tiny rear end. "Yes. Why did you lie?"

She stared down at her coffee, and when Melissa looked up, her deep brown eyes were filled with trouble. "I'd seen him in town. I never told you this, but I think that Walter was peeping on me the day that he fell from that tree. I know it sounds ridiculous. And I'm sorry to speak ill of the dead, I really am. But there were other times, when I'd be in our pool or sunbathing, that I swore that he was watching from your house."

Oh no. This was worse than I'd ever thought. "Melissa, I'm sorry to tell you, but I think that you're right. Walter was spying on you when he fell. He denied it, of course. But it's what led to our divorce."

"So I'm not crazy."

I grabbed her hand. "No, you're not. I'm sorry that I didn't tell you. But there was no good way to mention it."

"No, I suppose there wasn't." She stared into her coffee for another minute before straightening. "But anyway, I saw him here and wanted to talk to him, wanted to clear the air. Dennis didn't know a thing about it. He would've killed Walter if I ever told him what he'd done."

I quirked a brow. "He would have?"

"Yes, but he didn't," Melissa quickly added. "Anyway. I'd had Walter's number because of our neighborhood list."

The entire neighborhood had printed a sheet with people's numbers as a contact list. It had hung on my refrigerator for ages. "So you called him."

"I wanted to tell him that I knew what he'd done and that even though it was wrong, I'd forgiven him."

"Why didn't you do that way back when it first happened?"

"I don't know," she admitted. "Maybe because it was so fresh on my mind. I'm sorry. I don't have a better answer than that. So anyway, I phoned him."

"And what did you talk about?"

"The thing was, he didn't answer, and I didn't leave a message. I didn't want him to think that I wanted something, you know…"

Melissa didn't want Walter to think that she wanted to start something up with him—like an affair.

I could understand that. "So then what happened?"

She looked at me blankly. "Nothing. That was it. I called. He didn't answer, and that was the end of it. Nothing more. I didn't know anything else until folks said that he'd been murdered. And of course I read it in the paper."

"The paper?" There was a Willow Lake paper? "Where'd you get it?"

"I have a copy here." Of course she did. Melissa pulled a small local rag from her purse and handed it to me. "You can have it."

"Thanks."

She rose. "Sorry about Walter. I really am. But please don't tell

Dennis about my involvement. That I called him. He'd want to know why and would start asking a bunch of questions that could be uncomfortable for you—especially if you knew about Walter's…antics."

Wow. It wasn't even noon, and Melissa was already dishing out veiled threats. I wondered what she did before supper.

"Anyway"—she smiled sweetly—"it was good to see you, Paige. Take care."

Without another word, she left. With nothing else to do, I scanned the paper to see what the town of Willow Lake knew about Walter's murder.

The text was by rote. It said that Walter had been found dead, and then there was a brief interview with Cowan. As I read his words, I stopped and had to reread them.

Officer Cowan had this to say about the murder, the newspaper read. *"There is a guilty party here in Willow Lake. They know who they are. Their name starts with a P and ends with a g. They should be warned. We're looking closely at them."*

Oh God. He was talking about me, except he couldn't even spell my name correctly. And he'd told the entire town that I was a person of interest.

My phone rang again as the taste of sawdust filled my mouth. I glanced down at it. It was Cowan. Again. He must've known that I was thinking about him.

I couldn't keep dodging his calls. "Hello?" I said weakly.

"Ms. Provey, is that you?"

I rolled my eyes. "Yes, it's me."

"This is Officer Cowan."

"Yes, I know."

"Oh, you do? Is my voice that recognizable?"

"It's the Caller ID."

"Huh. Right. Anyway, I need you to come down to the station."

"You're not going to arrest me, are you?" I joked.

"Um. We'll just see about that when you get here."

Then he hung up. That was all he said.

Oh no. I was going to be arrested for a crime that I hadn't committed.

If I ran, then I'd look guilty. With no other choice, I rose and headed back to my car, wondering if I had time to drop the creamer off at the cabin before I was put in the pokey.

CHAPTER 19

I wasn't arrested, thank goodness. It turned out that Cowan had a few questions for me about the morning that Walter was murdered.

"Now think back real carefully," he said intently. "Do your best. I know this was a couple of days ago and most folks forget a lot of the little details, but was there anything strange that happened?"

It was hard not to roll my eyes. I mean, really. Did I look so stupid that I normally forgot things? I put on my best thinking face. "There's really nothing else that I remember."

"Okay," he said, disappointed. "Well, if you recall anything, let me know."

And that was that. Cowan let me go and I was grateful. I ran by the cabin to put my creamer in the fridge before it spoiled, and decided that I could afford something other than a tuna fish sandwich for lunch. Spending five bucks on food wouldn't kill the bank. And then I'd come back and write.

Just as I was about to leave, my phone rang. It was Madeleine. "Darling," she cooed, "I must have pages. I tried to put your editor off, but she's insisting."

My stomach clenched. I didn't think what I had was good enough to hand over, but what choice was there? "I don't know," I replied, doing my best to sound worried.

"I'm sure what you have is great. Send it all. I've got to give her something."

Madeleine hung up before giving me a chance to argue. *Well, all right then.* It only took a minute to send over the file. She'd hate it. I knew she would. Madeleine would probably read it and tell me to start over. Since my stomach had dropped to the floor, I decided that to distract myself, I would definitely go into town and grab a bite.

I knew just the place to take my mind off things.

When I walked into the restaurant, I spotted Ferguson behind the bar cleaning glasses. "Ah, lass. What brings you in?"

"The fact that you call me 'lass,'" I joked.

He smiled, making the corners of his eyes crinkle. "Well, to me you are. I'm old enough to be your dad, I'm sure. Anybody young enough to be my daughter is a lass in my book."

"I knew there was something about you."

He grinned. "Want a bite to eat?"

"Yes. I'm starving." He handed me a menu and returned with a glass of wine. "Had a feeling that you also wanted one of these."

"You'd be right." I sipped the white as my gaze picked over the menu. "I'll have the turkey club."

I should've been avoiding carbs, but bread every once in a while wasn't going to kill me. It would just make me fatter.

"Coming right up," he told me.

The door opened behind me, and I felt prickles on the back of my neck. Before I could turn to see who was causing the sensation, a hand was on my arm.

"I've been looking for you."

Grim stood all manly and stuff beside me. He gazed down at me with those piercing silver eyes of his, and a huge knot clotted up my throat and also smothered my brain with a blanket so that I couldn't think.

Finally I managed, "Oh? You were looking for me? Why?"

"Because we haven't finished our lesson."

I flapped my hands with excitement. "I have news about that."

He glanced at my waving hands, and I slid them between my thighs.

There was nothing sexy about looking like a bird. Unless it was a swan, and swans didn't flap their wings like they had Tourette's syndrome.

He slid onto a barstool in this really fluid movement that made me feel even more self-conscious about my alien fingers.

Ferguson came up. "Want a burger, Grim?"

"That would be great. Thanks."

Didn't Grim care about his arteries at all?

He turned those silvery eyes on me. "So. Tell me what you were going to say."

"Right. Well, Estelle came over and it turns out"—I leaned forward so that no one could hear—"that I'm a vegetation witch. That's why the fire spell didn't work when you tried it with me. Because I can't control fire."

I said it all so smartly that I didn't expect Grim's response to be, "That wasn't real fire, like I said before. It was an androgenous element. None of them."

"Well, I'm a vegetation witch. See that plant over there?" I pointed to a succulent on a table. "I'm going to make it grow."

It looked like he was biting back laughter. "Go for it."

I pushed up my sleeves because using magic meant I needed all the focus. All of it. I put my intention on the plant, letting that devil of a dragon uncoil in my belly and…nothing happened.

"Why is this happening to me today?"

"It's not you."

"Then what is it?"

He stared at me in a way that gave me the good kind of willies. "It's the magic."

"What do you mean, it's the magic? How does that even make sense?"

Grim pursed his lips. "I have a theory about your power."

"Would you like to share it with me?"

"Not until I'm sure."

I didn't like that answer. "Since we're talking about me and all, and since it's my power, it might be nice to know what you're thinking."

"No."

He was so infuriating. "If you had something wrong with you, I'd tell you. I wouldn't keep it a secret because secrets aren't nice."

"I'm not a nice person," he nearly growled.

What was it with him? He'd touched me on the arm when he arrived. *Touched me.* Like we were...intimately acquainted or something. And now he was brushing me off. Ugh. I didn't like him.

"Here's a news flash—you don't have to be nice to tell me what's going on with my magic. Stupid magic. I don't even like it anyway."

He laughed, which just burned me up even more. Grim must've seen that I was about to attack, because he said, "Settle down. I'll tell you when I'm ready." I needed him to be ready now. "There are a few more tests that I want to do."

"Tests? Like I'm a lab rat?"

His silvery eyes darkened. "The last thing you are is a rat."

His words put a large stone in my throat. "Okay," I managed to croak out.

He rose. "If you'll excuse me, I'll be right back."

Grim left for the bathroom, I supposed. Or maybe he made a quick jaunt down to the underworld so that he could confer with the devil himself about something. I didn't know and I didn't care. It wasn't my business.

"He likes you," Fergie said, depositing my club sandwich in front of me.

I nearly choked with laughter. "You must be joking. Likes me? You're not talking about old Grim Face, are you? Because the last thing he does is like me."

"No, he does. Trust me."

I cocked a brow at him. "Why should I trust you?"

"Because I've never seen him offer to give a woman magic classes. That isn't how Grim works. He's a loner. Likes to keep to himself."

"Burned in a past relationship, I've heard," I said before taking a bite of french fries. Boy, they were delicious—crispy and hot with just the right amount of salt. "That sort of thing will hurt a person bad."

"He was burned, yes, literally."

"I think Officer Cowan told me something about that."

Fergie just grunted, which suggested that I'd asked enough questions about it. Thinking it would be best to change the subject, I pulled my phone out of my pocket and flipped to a picture of Walter.

"The other night when I was here, did you see this man?"

Ferguson studied the picture for a long moment, scratching his graying hair. "Yes, I remember him pulling you outside."

"After that." Because I really didn't want to discuss that whole embarrassing scene. "Did he come back?"

"Yes, I believe that he did."

Victory! "Was he alone?"

Ferguson rubbed his jaw for about half a century and then finally said, "I think he was with a woman."

My heart skipped about a hundred beats. "He was? He was with a woman? Are you sure?"

"I think so. Tall, blonde." He thought a moment. "Yes. I'm almost certain that I saw him after you left, come back in with a lady. They sat in a corner booth and chatted with their heads together, very close. They might have even been playing footsy under the table."

Ugh. Footsy with Walter? Who was this woman that she was so desperate?

"Did you recognize her?" *Please, please say that you do.*

"Nope. Never seen her before in my life. But I'd know her if I saw her again."

That didn't help. I couldn't exactly go grabbing random blondes off the street and dragging them up to the bar for Fergie to study.

He leaned close. "But I will say this."

"What?"

"To me, she looked like a working girl, if you know what I mean."

"A prostitute," I screeched. Folks sitting at tables glanced over, and I clamped a hand over my mouth. "Sorry," I whispered, cheeks heating.

He waved away my concern. "Don't worry about it. But yeah, that was how she appeared."

Why would Walter have been with a prostitute? Okay, I knew *why*—to get some. But what did the prostitute have to do with his murder the next day? That would have been a one-night thing.

But you didn't take working girls out to dinner. So their relationship must've been more than simply hanging out in a bedroom. But had she been the one to do the deed? And why?

"Was she thin?" I asked.

"Most definitely. Quite thin. Quite tall."

So her butt print could match the one I'd found. If I could find her and get her to the cabin, I could compare.

"Is there anything else you can tell me about her?"

Ferguson nodded. "The hair. I don't think it was real. She was wearing a wig if I ever saw one."

A wig! Hmm. Melissa was tall, but she'd been adamant that she'd had nothing to do with Walter's murder. But she could have been lying. She might have slipped away from her husband long enough to have a quick meal with Walter.

But would she have been playing footsy with him? And why see him the next day?

I nibbled my bottom lip. Something about that didn't make sense. If Melissa had wanted revenge, she would have gotten it that night. She wouldn't have waited until the next morning.

But what if her husband found out and tracked Walter down? What if he'd done it and then somehow knew about the book and took that, too. It made sense. Sort of. Yes, it was reaching, I admit it, but it was the most plausible explanation so far.

Walter's murder and the book's disappearance couldn't be coincidence, like Grim had suggested.

Just as I was mulling all that over, he reappeared.

"How's your sandwich?" he asked.

I'd been so preoccupied I hadn't even tasted it. I took my first bite. "It's fantastic. Now. When do we have more lessons?"

CHAPTER 20

*W*e had our next lesson right after that. "So are you going to tell me what you think is going on with my power?"

"In a minute," he said, all serious-like.

He'd brought me to a spot by the lake that was lush with vegetation and mosquitoes, it turned out.

"Do you have any bug spray?" I showed him three welts. "They like my blood, and I forgot to armor up this morning."

Grim grabbed a packet of wipes from the box on his motorcycle, opened it and handed me one. I was tempted to ask if he'd rub the repellent on my skin, but knew that was going too far.

When I was done, I smiled. "I'm ready."

"I'm going to give you some of my power and see what you can do with it."

"Great." I guessed. I didn't know. "What's your power?"

"I can harness lightning."

"That sounds dangerous."

"It is. But most of us who harness magical creatures can."

"Is that like a personality trait? You know, it sort of goes with the territory?"

He nodded. "Something like that." He opened his palm and a bolt appeared. "We're going to play a game. I'm going to hand this to you, and you're going to hand it back."

So many questions. But I did as he asked. We stood close, really close, so close that I could feel his breath flickering my hair as he cupped his hands and then gently touched my hand, letting the ball fall into my palms. I held it for a few seconds and then concentrated as I let it drop back into his.

We did this for what felt like an hour. The whole while my skin jumped every time Grim touched me. I stared at my hands, too afraid to look up at him.

"How long are we going to do this?"

"Shh," he told me. "Focus."

All I could think about was how rough his hands were and how I was pretty sure I saw rippling muscles beneath his shirt. Not that I had X-ray vision, but his clothing kind of suctioned to him in spots and it was impossible *not* to notice.

Finally he retrieved the small ball of energy from me and squished it between his fingers. He took a few steps back, and I felt like I could breathe again.

"Now. I want you to try that."

"Try what?"

"Making lightning."

"But I don't know how."

"You also didn't know how to call vines."

"Good point." I nibbled the inside of my lip. "So just, like, call it."

"Yes," he said impatiently.

Just as I was about to do that, a tiny sound caught my attention. It reminded me of a baby bird calling for its mother.

"What's that?" I asked.

He stopped and listened. Ignoring me, Grim crossed to a bush and pulled back a branch. "What are you doing here?"

Curious, I padded over and followed his gaze until I spotted a hairless creature. It looked like a small living tree. "What's that?"

"This is a tree nymph. It's a baby. Left alone, it won't do well out here. If it doesn't die, it'll grow up to become a vengeful nymph."

"How vengeful?"

"Catastrophic. I need to find a place for it." Grim reached toward it, but the tiny nymph backed away. "It doesn't want to be caught. I'm going to take off my shirt. Can you turn around?"

I glanced to see if maybe he was talking to someone else. "You mean me?"

He rolled his eyes. "Yes, you. Can you turn around?"

Was he nervous about taking his shirt off in front of me? "Sure. Let me give you the privacy that you deserve."

"Thanks."

I tried really hard not to look. Promise that I did. But at the very last minute I peeked and caught a flash of Grim's torso. He had a long scar that ran down his back at an angle. It almost looked like a sword slash.

I turned around as Grim said, "Caught it."

"Oh good."

He put the nymph in the box on his bike and pulled his shirt on. His front was even more than I could have hoped for—all tanned, rippling muscles and Roman-godlike sinews.

I wiped drool from the bottom of my lip before he could notice. "So, what's it doing here?"

Grim made sure the travel box was secure and frowned. "I don't know. They're very rare in this part of the world. The only thing I can think is…"

"It came from the book," I said.

He nodded.

"You want it. I want to know who killed Walter. Do you have any leads? Any at all?"

Grim slowly nodded. "In fact, I do."

I hadn't expected him to actually have one or two. "Let's hear them."

"There's a woman who lives in town who has a penchant for magical creatures."

"A witch?"

"Yes," he said, sounding annoyed that he was even sharing this information with me. "But not a witch with creature abilities."

"Do you have to be born with that or something?" He grunted in response. "Never mind. What about her?"

"She's always wanted them. But a regular witch isn't allowed to have a permit for magical creatures."

"You need a permit?"

He stared at me blankly. "Of course. Like any wild animal. You have to have a permit to handle one."

"Who is this woman? What does she look like?"

"What does it matter?"

"What if she was the woman seen with Walter? What if she murdered him to get the book?" When he didn't say anything, I pressed on. "You have to take me to meet her. Tell her that she can help me learn magic. What sort of magic does she have?"

"She's a weaver."

"A weaver?"

He nodded. "Yeah."

I clapped my hands. "Perfect. Tell her I want to weave a tapestry or embroider a magical pillow or something. I'll feel her out because she'll be expecting you to be up to something—you know, with your connection to the police and everything."

He studied me for a long minute. "Do you think that you can do it? Feel her out?"

The lightning lesson forgotten, Grim led me to his motorcycle.

I could muddle my way through the thorniest of conversations. I'd done it plenty of times with my editor—telling her that I was almost finished with edits when I hadn't even started them. If I could pull the wool over her eyes, I could handle a simple weaver.

I COULDN'T HANDLE the simple weaver.

Actually, it wasn't her that I couldn't handle. It was the whole weaving thing.

Sanibel (I guessed her parents really liked the island) held out her hands. A cord-like thread wormed its way into the loom she held.

Her brown eyes sparkled. "Now, you do it."

Grim had done exactly what I'd asked. He'd driven me over to her house, explained who I was (a witch wanting to weave), and then he left. Me. Alone.

Sanibel had spiderlike dark eyes, glittering and chocolate-colored.

"Move the yarn up over the first thread and then down under the second. Repeat your pattern."

I sat with a loom on my lap and did as she said. "So," I said, trying to sound casual, "I saw my first magical creature the other day."

Way to be coy, right? But Sanibel didn't seem to notice. She spoke as she threaded the loom. "Aren't they wonderful? What did you see?"

I pretended to think about it. "Some sort of little creature. I think Grim called it a sprite, but I don't think that's right."

"A nymph?" Sanibel was practically salivating. "Is that what you saw? Not like that, dear, like this." She showed me how to work the yarn again. "What kind of witch did you say that you were again?"

"Oh, I'm a mphfrphm," I mumbled into the back of my hand.

Sanibel nodded as if she caught every word. "And you want to learn how to loom? Why's that?"

"Well, I'm thinking of majoring in it for my witch studies class."

"Aren't you a bit old for a witch studies class?" she asked, eyes suspicious.

"I've gone back to school. I spent some time being married."

"And raising children?" Sanibel nodded. "I understand that. We witches must stick together."

"I know," I said.

So Sanibel did sort of look like she could have been the woman that Ferguson was talking about. She had light hair and she was certainly tall and thin. But there was something rather nonsexual about her. She was all business, and I couldn't see her letting her hair down for five minutes to play footsy.

But that didn't mean she couldn't have.

"Not like that, dear," she instructed again. "Like this."

My yarn was all knotted. I was definitely not a weaving witch. "So you like magical creatures," I murmured.

"Don't we all?" Sanibel said, distracted with her own weaving.

"Do you know, you look familiar. Didn't I see you at the restaurant the other night? Friday, I think it was. Ferguson was bartending."

Sanibel shook her head. "I'm afraid that it wasn't me."

Not to be discouraged, I kept on. "I've heard that there's a magical book somewhere in town. It has a whole bunch of animals trapped inside. But they can be let out. Have you heard of such a book? Do you think something like that could exist?"

"Hmm? A book? Well, you'd have to ask Grim about that." Sanibel glanced around the living room with want. "I've always wanted to fill this house with little creatures, but I don't have the credentials, I'm afraid. So if there was a book like that..."

"You'd jump at the chance to get your hands on it?"

She frowned, her lips pouting out a bit. "No, I don't think so. Something like that could be quite dangerous if in the wrong hands."

"Well, I would think that someone might be interested in a book like that. Wouldn't you think so?"

She tied off the edges of her yarn and pulled the completed work from the loom. "See what I've done?"

My jaw unhinged. Sanibel's tapestry hung in the room like a work of art—splashes of color deep and jewel-toned. "Wow. How do you do that?"

The yarn shimmered and the scene was one of a man hunting a woman—probably a Greek god. It seemed those gods did a lot of woman hunting back in the day.

"I am a weaver," Sanibel said. "My talents lie in making scenes like this come to life." She snapped her fingers, and the man and woman jumped off the fabric. He chased her around the room while she shrieked in fear, or was she playing? The woman's eyes twinkled with mischief.

This was all theater, I realized.

The man, who was only covered in a towel at his waist, was just about to catch the woman when both figures disappeared and ended up back in the tapestry.

"Is it an illusion?"

Sanibel considered the question. "It doesn't have to be an illusion. It can be more than that for whoever witnesses it."

I frowned. "You could do a lot of mischief with magic like that."

"You can if you so want." She flicked her hand, and the tapestry zipped over to the wall and hung itself there. "Now. Tell me why Grim really dropped you off. It's not to learn to weave, is it? You're not a weaver." She stopped and stared at what I was doing. "Or are you?"

The yarn that I'd been fighting had settled down, and it was working through the loom on its own. As we watched, more and more yarn snaked its way through the thread until the small loom was filled with about a place-mat-sized tapestry. It was a picture of a book—the magic book. The one by Heronomous whoever—the tome that had changed my life.

"My girl, you might be a weaver yet." Sanibel took the yarn from the loom, snipped it off, and we watched the image of the book open and close. "What's that?"

"It's what changed me. I wasn't a witch until a few days ago, when that book hit me on the head."

She frowned, obviously not used to being told that magical books could plunk folks on the head and turn them into witches.

"That book only released what was already there. But what is it?"

"It..." Was I supposed to tell her this part? I made the decision without too much thought. "It's the one I was telling you about—a magical prison for people and creatures, and it's missing. I must find it."

She quirked a brow in amusement. "So that you can stop it from falling into the wrong hands?"

Sounded stupid when she put it that way. But it was what it was. "Yes. Have you seen it? Do you know where the book is?"

Sanibel shook her hands. "No, I don't." She regarded me for a moment and then threw her head back and laughed. "Did Grim tell you that he thought I might have it?"

"Er, no. Of course not."

She wagged a finger. "He's trying to be sly. He knows how much I love magical creatures. I do. That's the truth." She waved to the tens of tapestries on her walls. "But my talents don't lie in creatures. They lie in this—in the weaving. With it, sometimes I see the future. Sometimes I see options." Sanibel settled a keen eye on me. "Tell Grim that next time, if he wants information, he can come himself instead of sending his girlfriend."

I scoffed. "I'm not his girlfriend."

Her gaze started at my head and trailed to my feet and back up. "Right. Now. If you want tapestry-making lessons, I'm happy to help. Otherwise there's nothing else that I can tell you."

I paused. "You can see the future?"

She nodded. "In the tapestry."

"Can you ever see the past?"

"Sometimes. If it's mine, I can. But other people's can be more blurry. Why?"

"Never mind." I took my tapestry. "Thank you for your time."

It appeared that I had a bone to pick with Grim.

CHAPTER 21

"She doesn't have the book," I told him later.

"Too bad. I considered her a solid lead."

We were at my house. Grim had picked me up from Sanibel's, and I hadn't said a word to him, only hopped onto the back of his bike.

Besides, he hadn't deserved a word. He'd only left me at Sanibel's to get me out of his way.

So when we reached the cabin, I climbed off his bike and glared at him. That was when I told him about the book.

He clicked his tongue. "What a shame."

"No it's not. You wanted me out of your hair." However thick and luscious it might have been. "I don't understand you. One minute you take me out to lunch and appear human, or as close to it as I suppose a wizard who hunts creatures that eat witches can be; the next you're brushing me off. What's your problem?"

He smirked. "I don't have a problem."

"Yes, you do. Your problem is interfering with my life. I'm trying not to go to prison for a crime that I didn't commit, here. Don't you get that? I'm attempting to stay out of jail and rebuild my life after Walter ruined it. Do you even know what that's like? Every time you google your own name, you read a story about what a hypocrite you are, see memes of yourself fighting with a cat for some reason."

He frowned.

"A few months ago there was a set of memes with me and a cat arguing. People would always change the text." He kept staring at me blankly. "Forget it. But I'm just not into being told that I'm helping when all you wanted to do was drop me off with Sanibel so that I could watch her knit."

"Weave," he corrected.

"I don't care!" As soon as the last word was flung from my mouth, it happened. A bolt of lightning sprang from my fingers and zapped the seat of Grim's bike.

"Ouch!" He jumped up and glared at me, fuming.

"I'm sorry."

"You did that on purpose," he accused.

"No, I didn't. I don't even know *how* I did it."

But it happened again. This time, instead of hitting his seat, the lightning struck his leg.

"Stop it!"

"I'm not doing it on purpose." A bolt zipped from my hands again, and this time it struck his shoulder. "Oops."

It came out really weakly, sounding so pathetic that I knew he didn't believe it was an accident.

Fury alighted on Grim's face. It was all twisted with anger and rage. "If you want to play rough, I can play rough."

"I don't—"

I didn't have a chance to finish the sentence because the next thing I knew, he had his own bolt of power in his hand and was shooting it toward me.

Oh my gosh. He was going to kill me. I didn't know what to do, so I jumped to the right, out of range of his magic. I landed on the ground, hitting my shoulder on the earth.

My body groaned with pain. I was too old to be doing this crap.

And that ticked me off.

I didn't even know what I was doing at that point, but I opened my hand and a bolt appeared.

"Want to play?" Grim asked, a sexy sneer on his face.

"I told you it was an accident!" I threw the bolt, but he grabbed it from the air and tossed it back at me. The magic struck the earth at my feet. Dirt and grass exploded into the air, pelting me.

I was done playing nice.

"Had enough?" he mocked.

"Not by a long shot."

I grabbed another bolt of magic from the air and aimed it at his leg. Grim dodged it, rolling to one side. When he was up on his feet, he already had a bolt in his hand. He threw it at me, and I did the only thing that I could think of.

I ran.

I heard feet pounding behind me. He was chasing me! This was like the most warped game of tag I'd ever played.

"Didn't your mother tell you not to beat up girls?" I shouted over my shoulder.

"My mother isn't here, and she never met you."

How dare he insult me? "It was an accident."

"That last one was an accident, too?"

His voice was in my ear now. I glanced a quick look to see him directly behind me. "Okay, the last one wasn't, but the first ones were."

"That was what I thought."

He was going to kill me. I had no doubt. He would catch me and do something terrible. I had to stop him, so I grabbed another bolt and threw it over my shoulder.

"Ouch! Oh, you're getting it now."

The next thing I knew, I was tumbling to the ground, rolling in pine needles and dried brown leaves that had been on the earth probably since the creation of the planet.

Grim had me and was going to kill me.

"Don't hurt me," I yelped.

I was on my back, eyes closed. My arms were pinned to the ground. I didn't dare watch as he destroyed me.

But then he said in a low, husky voice, "Open your eyes."

I did and sucked air. He straddled me, silver eyes gleaming, his hair falling onto my face, one corner of his mouth tugging up in amusement.

The tension was thick. The humidity was ripe in the air, but there was an electricity oozing off him that zapped straight to every female organ in my body. All one of them. He leaned forward and I knew he was going to kiss me. We hadn't even had a date, but I'd been around long enough and had written about enough kisses to know when one was about to happen.

"What…what are you going to do with me?" I croaked.

He opened his mouth to say something and then stopped. He shook his head.

No, no! He was breaking the moment. Why?

Grim released my arms and got off me. I sat up and we stared at one another.

I was terrible at picking men. I was canceled. My life was a mess. I could speak to ghosts. I was a suspect in a murder.

But in that moment all I wanted was to feel Grim's lips.

So I lunged for him. I pressed my lips to his.

He didn't do anything.

Oh no. This had been a mistake. I'd completely misread the moment. I was about to break the kiss and apologize when his lips parted and his arms wrapped around me.

And we were kissing! My brain exploded. Every inch of me was on fire as the husky man tugged me toward him. I was suddenly tugging on his shirt and he was tugging on mine and I realized that I needed Grim more than simply to just go all the way.

I needed his help.

I pulled away first and stared at him. He stared at me and smiled—a genuine smile.

"That hurt, what you did back there."

"I didn't mean to. But I could weave, too. What's wrong with me?"

"There's nothing wrong with you," he said kindly.

"That's the nicest thing you've said to me. Ever."

He threw his head back and laughed. "I suppose that's true." Then Grim rose and offered me a hand. "Come on. There's something I want to show you."

Your bedroom? It was a decent question after how hot that kiss had been. His hand slid over mine, and sparks flew as our flesh touched.

I only released his hand when we reached the bike.

Snow stood outside the cabin. "You coming in?"

I mouthed behind Grim's back, *No.*

"He is fine," she told me.

131

Wow. Talk about a blast from the past. No one spoke like that anymore.

I hopped onto Grim's bike and did everything in my power not to press my nose to the back of his neck as we rode down the dirt path. We roared through town and reached a small cottage just on the outskirts. It sat on a slip of land that jutted out onto another part of the lake. The woods had claimed part of the home. Vines crept up the white siding, and long-stemmed flowers grew from boxes that hung from the windows.

"Where are we?" I asked after he killed the engine.

"My house."

"Your what?"

He smirked. "My home. Don't worry, I didn't bring you here to kill you. Or jolt you with magic," he added with humor in his eyes.

I felt my cheeks redden. Then what were we doing here?

He opened the front door, and as soon as we walked in, I sucked air. The place was immaculate and quite masculine. The living room was framed out in dark oak that was polished glossy. The furniture was nice. He even had a pair of leather-covered Chesterfield chairs that must've cost half a fortune.

He leaned over and his hand grazed mine. Tingles moved all over my body as he said, "What do you think?"

"I think you have more taste than I ever gave you credit for."

Grim smiled. "Come on. There's more."

I followed him past the living room to the back of the house where there was an attached solarium or indoor greenhouse or something like that. It was at least two stories tall, covered in glass and plants.

"This was created by magic, wasn't it?"

He nodded. "Yes."

"You did this?"

"My mother."

I couldn't quite imagine the woman that had birthed Grim. "Where is she?"

"Dead now several years," he murmured, hurt in his voice. "But she created this."

Before another word escaped his lips, a huge doglike creature bounded out of the plants and raced to Grim.

"Savage, there's a good boy." The thing licked Grim before stopping in front of me and pausing. Grim gave him a scratch behind the ears. "He's a winged dog."

I frowned. "Winged dog? I've heard of winged horses and lions, but not dogs."

"Yeah, that was the problem. His mother rejected him, so that's how he ended up here."

That was when I noticed that from behind the plants little heads poked out. Some were humanlike; the others resembled animals.

"This is what you do with them? The creatures that you catch?" I asked.

Savage pressed his nose to my hand and I patted him. "He likes you," Grim said. "But to answer your question, no. These are the orphans, those abandoned to grow up on their own. So I've taken them in."

One of the creatures, a little stick-looking fellow with leaves sprouting from its head, ran up to Grim and jumped on his arm, crawling up his shoulder to rest.

"There, there, little one," he said gently.

Like, I really had no words. How was this rough-and-tumble man so gentle, so kind? He'd shot lightning bolts at me. Of course, that was after I'd shot him.

"Want to hold him?" Grim asked, taking the little guy from his shoulder and offering him to me. "He likes to curl up in your hand."

"Sure." I opened my fingers, and the little tree fellow stared at my palm a moment before slowly climbing up my wrist and into my hand. His feet tickled as he made his way to the cup of my palm and curled up to sleep. After a few moments I said, "What do I do now?"

Grim smiled. "Let's put him up."

Ever so tenderly, Grim scooped up the creature and placed him back in a sea of trees that swallowed him up.

"Do you feel safe with all these creatures here?" I asked.

He nodded. "There are protection spells put into place, to keep me safe."

"Did you do them?"

He shook his head. "No. My mother did."

"What sort of witch was she?"

Grim patted Savage and then took my hand and led me from the room. Savage followed us into the house proper, and Grim closed the doors to the greenhouse.

He dropped my hand but brushed his against it again as he moved past me. "Care for something to drink?"

"Water?"

"I can do that. Have a seat. I'll be right there."

Savage followed me as I sat in one of the Chesterfields. The winged dog sprawled out beside me, his head in his paws.

Grim appeared and handed me a bottle of water. He had one for himself, and he sat in the opposite chair. "So. Why did I bring you here?"

"Yes, I'd like that answer."

"I think the answer to what sort of witch you are can be found in this house."

I unscrewed the bottle and took a long pull of water. "Okay," I replied, not at all understanding what he meant. "So what's the answer?"

"You're like my mother."

Great. Grim had mommy issues and wanted me to be his mother. "And how's that?"

"You had vine magic the night the scree attacked. I assumed that you'd just seen Estelle?"

"Um, yes, I had."

"And you told me that you'd been able to weave a tapestry after spending time with Sanibel. Right?"

I nodded.

"And you had lightning power after riding with me."

"Yes yes yes."

He scrubbed a hand down his cheek. "Paige"—I shuddered at the sound of my name on his lips—"you are an absorber."

I squinted. "What?"

"You can take on the powers of those you're around. You are among one of the rarest witches ever born."

CHAPTER 22

I looked at Grim for a long moment and then laughed. "An absorber? I'm a rare witch? You had me for a second there. But I don't believe you. I know that everyone wants to think they're special, but this is too much."

He studied me with an expression that I couldn't place. Maybe he was wondering why I wasn't believing his bullcrap. "I'm telling you what I think. My mother had the same ability. Whoever she was around, she took on their powers. She told me that as a teenager, when she was figuring out what kind of witch she was, it was nearly impossible to pin down because of that."

"I'm hardly a teenager."

"I know that you're close to my age."

I didn't even bat an eyelash. "Exactly. So..."

"You're a late bloomer," he said.

I laughed. "A late bloomer? Is that what you call it?"

"Yes," he told me so pointedly I pursed my lips shut.

"Now, I don't know exactly how to train you. But I can figure it out. There are a few old witches here who helped my mother when she was coming up."

I opened my mouth to argue, but who was I kidding? I nearly shot his face off with a bolt of electricity. I needed help and I needed training. Clearly I couldn't do it myself. And since I didn't know any witches, I would have to rely on Grim for help.

I wondered if that meant we would kiss again. I kind of wanted that really badly even though it was the last thing I needed.

"Okay, so we find someone who can properly teach me not to kill people with magic. I'm all for it."

"Good."

There was a long pause. "Don't you have something else to tell me?"

He quirked a brow. "Do I?"

"About my ex-husband's death."

"I don't think so."

I glared at him. "I thought that was why we came here."

"We came here so that you could see what your magic can do." He glanced toward the closed doors of the greenhouse. "That you can build, create with your fingertips."

And I also had a book to get to my agent. How could I possibly do it all?

"Thanks," I murmured, but I noticed that Grim was watching me with a twinkle in his eyes while he lightly drummed his fingers on the wooden arm of the Chesterfield. "You're toying with me, aren't you?"

"I would never do that."

"You like to work alone. It's a thing with you. You don't trust easily."

His brows rose to peaks. "Is that so?"

I nodded. "I study people for a living. That's what authors do."

"They do?"

"We do. And you are textbook. So. You dropped me off at Sanibel's house to get rid of me—so that you could have time alone. To do what?"

He stopped drumming his fingers and raked his hands down his face. "There is a small ring in Willow Lake."

Now he had my attention. "What kind? Drugs?"

"Prostitution."

I tsked. "And it's such a nice community."

"That's why it's very small. They're good about keeping things quiet. But I believe your ex wound up meeting one of the prostitutes."

"And things went wrong?" I had a hard time buying it. "Walter was at the cabin."

"I heard that Walter was seen the night before his murder with a woman," he told me.

So he'd been asking around. "Right. I already know that—Ferguson told me about a woman." An idea came to me. "I also spouted off about the book outside the restaurant."

"So the person who killed Walter might have asked him to meet up again. You don't take a prostitute out to eat."

"So what does the prostitution ring have to do with anything then?" I asked.

Grim ran his palms over the glossy wood on the chair, thinking. "I think Walter got an escort, someone higher paid but still a prostitute. That's why no one has come forward and said that they were dating him. I believe they found out about the book when you said something about it and talked Walter into taking them out to where you were staying at the cabin. Walter was good at tracking you down, right?"

"He was. He found Patricia and got her to open the cabin for him."

"He probably asked around until he figured out who was renting to you. Then he went out there, with the woman—she may have used some pretense that they would really get some sort of revenge on you by screwing around at the cabin while you were gone. Then when she got her hands on the book, she killed him."

"But why end his life?"

"I don't know. Maybe they got into an argument about it and she pretended to put the book away. Then realizing that he wouldn't let her take it, she did the deed."

Grim had been very sneaky this whole time. "Why are you helping me?"

Grim laughed. "Isn't it obvious?"

I shrugged. "Not to me."

He shook his head and rose. Offered his hand again. "Come on. Let's get you back to the cabin."

Alarmed, I said, "Wait. You've been running around this whole time investigating. I want to help."

"Paige"—one again those fissures of electricity snapped down my spine—"this is dangerous work. I don't think you get that."

"I get it. I was almost eaten by a scree, in case you don't remember."

"This isn't the type of thing that you need to get involved with. I can help you. But you need to stay put. Let me do my work."

His fingers trailed down my arm, and my legs became slippy noodles. "But—"

"No buts. We're talking about a murderer. Someone very dangerous. They've killed once. They won't think twice about killing again."

I stared at him for a long minute, trying to decide on a response, but nothing came.

"Do you want to go out sometime?" he asked.

I nearly collapsed to the floor. "You mean, like a date?"

"That's generally what's implied when someone asks another out."

"Oh, right. Sorry, my brain's..."—*totally frazzled because of your hotness*—"tired. But yes, that sounds great. I would like that."

"Good. But first, let me get this settled. Let me work with the police to catch whoever killed Walter. We'll clear your name."

"Thanks," I said, still trying to wrap my head around the fact that we were going out on a date. I was going out with this Greek-god-looking guy. And he thought that I was in my thirties!

That was all I could think of as Grim took me back to the cabin and dropped me off.

As soon as he was gone, Snow appeared. "So, did you do the nasty?"

I frowned. "No, we did not. We didn't even come close. He was too busy telling me about a prostitution ring in town."

She folded her arms. "What about it?"

"That he thinks Walter was with an escort the night he was murdered. That didn't surprise me. I'd heard that before."

"What did surprise you?"

I considered that. "Well, I guess it surprised me that—"

My phone rang and I pulled it from my purse. "Hello?"

"Paige, is that you?" My sister's thick Southern drawl pierced the receiver. "Can you hear me?"

"Yes, Cammie. I can hear you. You okay?"

"No, I am not okay. Where you at?"

"Willow Lake. I'm staying at a cabin."

Cammie breathed heavily into the phone. "I need a place to stay, Paige. I need someplace to crash for a little while."

Most sisters would probably say yes, absolutely, I'll help you. But my sister, Cammie, tended to bring trouble with her everywhere she went. She was one of those women who suffered from a prolonged adolescence—the sort that never ended.

She always had a new boyfriend, went out to bars every night, and basically was an expert at making a mess of her life.

I didn't need her here.

"Cammie, do you need money?"

"No, I don't need money. I need to see you. Had a dream that you needed help."

My brow wrinkled. "I thought you wanted a place to stay."

"That too."

I rolled my eyes. "Look, this isn't a good time."

Her voice cracked with static. "What'd you say?"

"I said this wasn't a good time."

"It's a good time." I started to protest, but she cut me off. "Where are you on Willow Lake?"

My chest tightened with worry. The last thing I needed was Cammie bringing more drama into my life. "I said it's not a great time. Listen, Cammie. Why don't you tell me where you are, and I'll see if I can get someone out there to help you?"

"The connection's bad," she said. "Can't hear you. I'll call back."

She hung up and my hopes sank. If I thought things were a mess now, if Cammie arrived, they'd get even worse. Somehow whenever her hands touched a situation, it went from bad to the worst disaster ever known to man.

Like the one time when Cammie wanted to make her own prom dress. She was a couple years older than me and enlisted my help in creating said gown. She spent weeks sewing and ruffling and attaching tiny flowers onto the thing. When it was all said and done, the dress was beautiful. The skirt was shorter in the front than in the back, coming just to the knee.

She showed her friends and they all wanted her to make them dresses, too. So she had me help her. Well, we were so busy putting together dresses that we forgot to make sure we were putting the shorter length in the front. When prom night came and her friends tried on their gowns, they realized the fatal mistake—they were shorter in back, coming up to their knees.

The dresses just looked awful, but there was nothing that could be done. It was too late.

And Cammie blamed me for the entire fiasco.

For months on end her friends were mean to me, teasing and embarrassing me every chance they had.

Cammie never did one thing to stop them.

And when my sister grew up and left the house, she was always back every few months needing this or that from my parents, who never cut her off until they died. Then she took the inheritance and blew through it.

And I supposed Cammie thought I was loaded, which was why she needed me now.

Well, I would put a stop to that. I dialed the number she had called from, but it went straight to voice mail.

I didn't have to worry. I was certain that Cammie wouldn't find me.

"Everything okay?" Snow asked.

"Yeah." I headed toward the house. "Come on."

"What are we doing?"

I turned back and smiled. "Why, we've got an escort to find."

There was no way that I was going to let Grim have all the fun. No. This was my life. If anyone was going to locate Walter's killer, it was going to be me.

Even though I had no idea how to go about it, I was a writer. I was creative.

I would come up with something.

CHAPTER 23

"Does this look hookerish?" I asked Snow.

"Only if hookers wear cashmere and pearl earrings," she said, her voice thick with doubt.

"Darn. I have absolutely nothing that screams 'hooker.'" I stared at the closet full of clothes. I mean, it was bad when you thought cashmere could be mistaken for cheap clothing that could easily come off. If anyone so much as popped a button on that piece, I'd be ticked.

Snow laid on the bed, her arms draped over the edge. "Let's face it. You have nothing that looks appropriate. Besides, do you really think that Mr. Fine would have made out with you if you did?"

My lips tingled at the thought of my kiss with Grim. Man, all I wanted to do was keep kissing him, but there were more important things to focus on.

I sat on the bed, feeling deflated. "How am I going to do this? What do I think, I'm just going to find a corner where the hookers hang out in Willow Lake? This is a family community. Not some seedy part of town."

"Every town has their seedy parts," she told me.

I lifted an eyebrow. "They do? Even here?"

"Of course." Snow rolled over. "Not that I would know about them, of course. It's not like I ever went there, but my brother used to."

It was far-fetched to think what was seedy twenty years ago would still be sketchy now. "Where was that?"

"There's a bar just outside the limits. Everybody knew that if you wanted to get high, that was the place to go."

"And you think this might be where I'd find prostitutes? Women willing to talk to me about who Walter could have been with?"

"Maybe," she said. "Couldn't hurt, now could it?" Snow sat up and scrutinized me. "But first, we need to find something for you to wear. Put a lot of makeup on and I'll be back."

"What are you going to get?"

She shrugged. "Hooker clothes. What else?"

Then she slid through the wall and disappeared.

I looked at myself in the mirror. My jawline was still somewhat strong, but if I peered closely, I spotted a little dip just outside my chin. I also had a couple of sunspots that needed correcting.

I was going to be the oldest-looking hooker ever. If there was any remedying my appearance, I needed to get started.

Twenty minutes later my face looked the part of a biker chic. Dark eyeliner rimmed my eyes, and I'd accentuated my lids with dark brown eyeshadow. My brows had been lined and brushed, and the blush on my cheeks was dark and striking.

My face was perfect.

Now all I needed were clothes.

Snow slid through the wall. "Ta-da! I've got clothes."

Her hands were empty. "You're not holding anything."

Her face scrunched up in puzzlement, but then she slapped her forehead. "Of course. They're on the other side of this wall. They couldn't come with me."

I walked outside and found some crumpled clothing. "Let's see how you look."

Turned out, Snow had a great eye for hooker clothes. Like, amazing. She'd found me a short black skirt and a tiny black top that, paired with a jean jacket, looked perfect.

After I teased up my hair, I became the part. "All right. You ready?"

Snow put on a pair of ghostly sunglasses for some strange reason. "Let's do this."

~

"I WANT TO LEAVE," I said, standing outside the bar. Snow was beside me, hovering for moral support.

"You can do it," she whispered.

"No, I can't. I'm here now and I can't."

A steady stream of men, tall, burly biker-looking men, were heading into the bar that was called the Hook and Anchor. This was some sort of fisherman's bar. Probably the sort of place that women disappeared from all the time. My life was in danger here. I'd walk in and never walk back out.

What was I doing?

"You want to know who killed Walter, don't you?"

"Yes," I muttered through clenched teeth.

"Then this place should have answers."

But if it had answers, wouldn't Grim have already figured them out? Wouldn't he have checked this place and discovered everything there was to know already? Would I just find out what he already knew?

"I can't." I turned around and Snow blocked my path. "What?"

"You're not a coward. You're a witch and a medium. So you've got more power in your pinky than anyone inside."

"But I don't know how to use my powers."

"You'll be fine. Just go in. Stop thinking about it and do it."

She was right. I took a deep breath and headed in.

The bar reeked of beer and sweat. Led Zeppelin played on the juke-box, and the voices were loud as people talked. The sound of pool balls cracking came from the back.

The crowd was thick, and the bar was buzzing. If I was going to do this, I needed some liquid courage.

"What're you having, doll?" came a husky voice.

"Shot of Jameson," I said.

The bartender—a pretty woman who looked like she'd read the same *Glamour* magazine as me on how to do makeup—poured the drink and pushed it over.

I paid and watched the crowd.

All the women in the place were tall—really tall, and their hair was perfect and their makeup didn't have one flaw.

Snow stood beside me. "This is a strange bar."

A voice came from the barstool to my right. "You look like you've seen a ghost, darling."

A dark-skinned woman with blonde hair had spoken. I smiled. "Not a ghost."

"First time here. You got that look," she said. "What're you doing visiting this place? This isn't exactly your side of town."

I was confused. This wasn't an African American bar. The crowd was clearly racially mixed. What did she mean? Then I realized that her voice was husky and her facial features were very well-defined. She had the best bone structure I'd seen in ages. I glanced at the bartender. She'd had a husky voice as well. Her features were also very defined. And all the women were tall.

Then it hit me. This was a trans bar.

Oh my goodness. I'd gotten this whole thing very wrong. Very, very wrong.

Or had I?

What if there was a prostitution ring in Willow Lake, but it was coming out of this bar?

I had to go for it. I said to my seatmate, "If a man wanted a date, could he get one here?"

She lifted one perfectly (and when I said perfectly, I mean perfectly) penciled brow. "A date? You mean, one that you pay for?"

"Um, yes."

She rested the backs of her toned arms on the bar and nodded. "There are a few who do that sort of thing. But most of us don't."

Cha-ching! She'd just said the magic words. I quickly pulled out my phone and found a picture of Walter. "Does he look familiar?"

"Let me see." She took a close look at the phone and thought about it. "I've seen him before. He was here the other night."

"Was it Friday?" I hated to put words in her mouth, but...she might need some help remembering the day.

"It may have been. Honey, so many people come and go in this place it's hard to remember. But I do recall him. I just can't say more than that."

Snow spoke. "Could it have been that Walter came in here, found a date and left?"

"I'm Chi-chi," the woman said. "And you've got a shell-shocked look on you. That must be your boyfriend or something, am I right?"

"He was my ex-husband."

Chi-chi nodded. "You're wondering how you never knew that he liked trans women, aren't you? Because that's all that's in this bar. Except for you, of course. And most are shape-shifters, but not all."

Chi-chi pointed and I followed her finger to some women who did indeed look a bit more feminine than she did, a feature they must have created with magic.

"Everyone's got their secrets," she said. "Everyone. You never know what someone's into until you know *who* they're into." She gave me a pointed look. "If you know what I mean."

"I guess I do. But tell me—since you recognize him, did you see who he was with? Do you remember anything?"

"Yeah, I remember a little bit. I think he was with Thelma."

My heart jumped. "Thelma. Who's Thelma?"

Chi-chi scanned the bar. "I don't see her. But you can always find Thelma at the ice cream shop this time of night if she's not here. She'll be by later."

I nearly kissed Chi-chi. "Thank you."

She watched as I gathered my purse. "You leaving so soon?"

"Yes. Sorry. I've got things to do." Like catch a murderer.

"Well, it was nice meeting you. Next time, don't bring the ghost."

My jaw dropped. Snow and I exchanged a look. "You can see her?"

"Honey, not everyone in this town is blind to ghosts. But be careful —those ghosts find out about you, and they'll be knocking on your door, trying to get you to solve all their problems."

I recalled the day that they'd nearly accosted me on the street. Without Snow's help, I would've been run over by my friendly neighborhood spirits.

"Thank you again," I told Chi-chi.

"See you around," she said as I scampered away and through the door.

Snow talked the whole way to the SUV. "So you think that this Thelma is at the ice cream shop right now?"

"That's what Chi-chi said." I hit the button on my key fob, and it bleeped as the doors unlocked. "I don't think she would lie to us."

"I don't either."

We got in the vehicle, and I sat with my hands on the steering wheel, glancing out the window. "So we go to the ice cream shop and check out the lead. We, or I guess, me—act really coy and just want some ice cream."

"Meanwhile you'll ask this Thelma if she's seen Walter. You show her Walter's picture and gauge her reaction."

"Right." I ran my hands down the leather-wrapped wheel. "I'll also check out her appearance—see if she's got blonde hair and a tiny butt."

"The most important thing," Snow agreed.

I couldn't believe it. I was so close to victory that I could almost taste it on my tongue. Me! Six months ago I'd been at my lowest point. And even when I'd arrived here in Willow Lake, I was still at the bottom of the emotional well, trying to pick up the pieces of my life.

But now I felt powerful, ready to go.

"You're nervous, aren't you?" Snow said.

I dropped my head. "Is it that obvious?"

"To me, but only because I've been spending time with you." She faced me. "You can do this. I regret now that I didn't fight hard enough to stay alive. If I had, I would've seen my kids grow up."

"You have kids?" I said, flabbergasted.

"I was a housewife. Yes, I had kids. But I don't know where they are."

"We need to rectify that," I said. "We've got to find them. As soon as this is over, I'm going to help you. We'll figure out who put you into that book, and we'll find your family."

Her ghostly hand covered mine. "Thank you."

"You're welcome."

"But I didn't say all of that so that you'd feel pity for me. I told you because deep down, Paige, you're a fighter. No one becomes a successful author without fighting for it."

"I haven't felt like much of a fighter lately."

"How could you? You were unplugged."

I frowned. "Unplugged?" Wait. I got it. "Oh, you mean *canceled*. Yes, I was. It was hard."

"Well, you're not canceled in my book." She smiled brightly. "To me, you've been renewed for another season."

She was right. I was uncancelable. Everything that I had done up to now proved it. I was resilient and I could, darn it, find Walter's killer and clear my name.

And I was going to do that right now.

CHAPTER 24

The ice cream shop had only one light on when we arrived. It made the place look creepy. Well, it was creepy since they kept dead bodies in the freezer.

At the same time it also fit since they served blood ice cream.

What sort of town was I living in, again?

"Okay, we'll go in, and Thelma won't see me," Snow said, going over the plan that she'd made up on the way over. "I'll go to the back and try to find her purse, see if I can get a full name and address."

"Then we'll take that name to the police," I relayed. "And get out of there."

"Yep. We'll hand the investigation over to them," she said.

I nodded. This was a good, simple plan. It would work and it would also keep me from getting into any danger. Snow would be doing the majority of the dirty work.

"Ready?" I said.

"Ready," she told me.

We got out of the car, and I took a deep breath before entering the shop. "Hello," I called.

"Hello," a masculine voice said. Tommy's head popped up from behind one of the ice cream cases. "How're you?"

My hopes sank. Thelma was supposed to be here. Now I had to

make up some excuse for coming in. Or...I could just talk to Tommy about her.

"Is Thelma here?" I asked.

Tommy shook his head. "No, she won't be in until later."

"Oh, okay." Now I had no idea what to do. "Thanks."

"Want some ice cream?" Tommy asked. "I was just about to put out another container of butter pecan. Your favorite."

It *was* good and I was suddenly very hungry. "Sure."

He smiled. "Let me just get it."

"What do we do now?" Snow asked.

I shrugged. Had no clue. The freezer clanged like it had the first time I'd arrived. The sound prompted a memory. I pulled Walter's phone from my pocket and listened to his messages. It was the same sound! It *was* Thelma who'd killed Walter. I had to tell the police. Forget getting her driver's license info. But first I needed to let Tommy know that I was leaving.

I moved behind the counter and saw a black purse, and sitting atop the purse was a blonde wig. Maybe Thelma was here and he was covering for her.

With Tommy out of sight, I quickly inspected the women's and men's bathrooms, but they were empty. There was probably an office in the back, so I sneaked behind the counter and opened the only door that didn't look like a freezer. My suspicions were confirmed because it was an office, but it sat empty.

"Paige," Snow said. "You have to see this."

She hovered above the purse holding a wallet. I moved over to her and gasped.

The picture was Tommy's. Which meant the wallet and purse and wig were also his.

Why hadn't I figured this out before? Tommy was Thelma. He wasn't trans. He was a shape-shifter. The truth had been staring me in the face for days; I just hadn't realized it.

I had to get out of there. I had to tell the police. Here I was, thinking that I'd meet Thelma and be all coy and everything. But when push came to shove and I was staring down at the face of a murderer, I was terrified.

My heart skittered in my chest. My stomach coiled. I suddenly had to use the bathroom, and we weren't talking number one. I was a cold, cold mess.

"What are you doing?"

Tommy stood outside the freezer, holding a big frozen cylinder of ice cream.

Um, holding your wallet, didn't seem like an appropriate reply. But I did have the good sense to drop the wallet and say, "Sorry. I was just…"

And then I ran toward the front door. All I had to do was get out of there and I'd be free. I reached the front door and pulled.

But it was locked.

I whirled around to see Tommy looming toward me. "We can lock the door from the inside. Just in case a bunch of rowdy vampires frenzy at the scent of blood ice cream."

This was bad. This was very, very bad.

"I'll go get help," Snow said before disappearing through the wall.

What sort of help was she going to get? No one could see her! Except Chi-chi. Maybe Snow could go back to the bar and tell Chi-chi that I was in trouble.

I just had to stay alive long enough for the ghost to return. Which meant that I had to win this confrontation with Tommy.

In every book that I'd ever written, when there was a confrontation with the killer, my heroine always found out the reason why the killer had committed murder.

So that was just what I would do—keep Tommy talking. Try to get him monologuing.

"Why'd you kill Walter?"

He smirked. "Figured it out, did you?"

"It wasn't easy."

Tommy wasn't holding the ice cream anymore. He had his hands clasped in front of him. They were big, strong hands.

"Walter stiffed me," he confessed.

I balked, waited. "He stiffed you?"

"Yeah. The night we went out. He didn't pay."

"Wait a minute." Had I heard him right? "The reason you killed my ex-husband was because he didn't pay you?"

Tommy rolled his eyes. "Are you deaf? Yes."

I pressed a hand to my head. "I'm so confused. I don't understand any of it."

"Uh," Tommy said, annoyed. "Fine. I'll explain everything. Walter picked me up at the bar Friday night. I'm trying to earn money for college. Like I told you. We ate some supper at the restaurant after your fight. My time is precious, and Walter knew that, but he didn't pay up after we went back to his motel. He promised that he had to get money from you. So I thought, okay, I'll wait. Well, the next morning I came back to the motel and told him that I needed my money then. He said, fine, let's go to your cabin. He found out the location and I drove. I didn't trust the man. Didn't want him in control. When we got there, he wanted to have some fun, so we started in. But then he hit me. Over the head with something hard. He said that he wasn't ever going to pay me, that I was trash. He was going to kill me," Tommy told me.

It was hard *not* to believe Tommy's story—there was a ring of truth to it. Walter could be mean.

"So I grabbed the closest thing possible," he said, continuing. "The knife. I pushed him into the bedroom and stabbed him. I was so scared that I ran out of there, forgetting the money that he owed me." He paused, seeming to think. "You know, you and me—we're not so different."

Yes, we were.

He continued. "You wanted Walter gone. That was obvious. You even said so. I did you a favor. I did a lot of people a favor. He was never going to pay. He attacked me. Attacked *me*. He was a horrible person and deserved what he got. You should be thanking me."

I thought about that. "There's one thing that bothers me."

"What's that?" Tommy asked.

"You said that Walter hit you over the head. Well, when he was found in bed, the rest of the cabin was untouched. There was no sign of struggle. Which, there would have been if your story were true. The place would have been a mess if you fought. But it wasn't. You simply killed him, and I don't doubt that he might have stiffed you. But I think you did it for a different reason."

"What's that?"

"Because you enjoyed it. I think my ex stiffed you, and you wanted revenge so you lured him to the cabin—he may have said that he would get money from me, and while you were there, you seduced him, told him to head into the bedroom, and then you murdered him."

Tommy's expression remained blank, which suggested I was wrong.

"Either that," I said, "or you knew about the book. Heard me yelling about it and you got Walter to take you to the cabin so that you could steal it. Once you disposed of Walter, you got the book and left."

Tommy frowned. "What book?"

"The one filled with magical beings and creatures."

He shook his head. "I have no idea what you're talking about. You were right the first time."

My jaw dropped in surprise. "I was?"

He nodded.

Oh my gosh! I'd guessed right. I'd totally and completely figured out who had killed Walter and the why and how. I should have been patting myself on the back. Cool and the Gang's "Celebrate" should have been blasting over the speakers. Confetti and balloons should have rained from the sky.

But my good feelings were cut short when Tommy unclasped his hands and pulled a rope from his pocket. "You've done good. Too good. And I'm afraid—"

Ugh. I knew where this was going. "Let me guess. I have to die."

He nodded. "Exactly."

Crap. And Snow wasn't even back with reinforcements.

CHAPTER 25

This was serious. I supposed that went without saying. But it was more serious than I'd even considered. Tommy had killed my ex simply because he wanted to.

That meant Tommy derived some sort of sick pleasure from murder.

Even worse, that meant he would get enjoyment from killing me, too.

"Let's just get this over with," he said, coming toward me with the rope taut between his outstretched hands.

"I don't think so." But where would I go? The door behind me was locked. The way in front of me was barricaded by Tommy himself.

If there was ever a time when I needed to use magic, it was then. I dug deep, trying to feel the power coiled in my belly.

I did this as I backed away from Tommy, who kept coming closer. Wasn't he worried that someone would want ice cream?

The dragon in my belly unfurled, and a surge of magic rocked my entire body. It was like trying to hold back a wall of water. The force was so much bigger than me that it spouted out like a geyser.

With my body flooded with magic, I raised my hands, waiting for a pulse of electricity to shoot from my fingers and smack Tommy in the face.

But that didn't happen. Tommy paled. His grip on the rope loosened. "What? What are you doing? Stop it!"

"What are you talking about?" I caught a glimpse of myself in the reflection from the windows and gasped. I looked like Walter!

My mind raced. Tommy was a shape-shifter. I was near Tommy, so I was taking on his powers.

And I had become his victim. Time to play this up. "Why'd you kill me? Why did you do it?"

"No," Tommy protested. "You're not real. None of this is real."

"You didn't have to kill me." I took a step forward as Tommy cowered. "I never hurt you."

Tommy bent at the knees. "Stop it."

I felt myself change again. When I looked in the reflective glass that lined the front of the shop, I was another man, this one a little shorter than Walter and balder. My heart thundered in my ribs. There had been more than one victim.

"No," Tommy shrieked.

"Why'd you kill me?" I demanded. "I was happy in my life."

Not sure if that was true, but it sounded good.

"Stay away!"

Tommy had his knees pinned to the floor now. I hovered above him. All I had to do was grab the rope and all his power would be gone.

"You killed me," I yelled, trying to sound big and scary. "You hurt me, and for that, you have to pay."

Tommy blinked. Anger flashed bright in his eyes, and his lower lip set into a firm line. "No, I don't."

He leaped forward, tackling me. My back hit the floor, and the air was knocked from my lungs.

Oh God. I was going to die. I just knew that I would. I couldn't get any air in. I couldn't exhale.

This was terrible. Was this how it felt to get the wind knocked out of you? If so, I never wanted to experience this again. It was horrible.

"Now you die!"

Well, those words brought the air rushing to my lungs. Tommy had the rope wound around my neck, and he started to pull.

The rope burned. I clawed at it, but Tommy pulled tighter. I felt myself change again, and this time I knew who I was. I stared up at Tommy as he pulled, and I mouthed, *Stop killing.*

He jerked back and released his grip on the rope. It fell to the ground and I coughed. It ticked me off what he'd done, trying to kill me.

Another rush of power worked through me, and the next thing I knew, an electric bolt fired from my hands and hit Tommy, sending him crashing against the wall.

He slumped to the floor, and I sighed with relief. I was about to check him for a pulse when a loud crash made me jump. I whirled around to see the glass covering the door shattered, Grim standing in the threshold.

He cocked a questioning brow my way. Right. I still looked like Thelma, Tommy's alter ego and killer extraordinaire.

The shifter power washed down my body like water, and I regained my identity.

"Paige." Grim strode forward and reached out as if he was going to hug me, but stopped.

I supposed we hadn't reached the hugging part of our relationship yet. Wasn't kissing past the hugging stage? Shouldn't he have hugged me?

He took my hand. "Are you all right?"

"I'm fine. Tommy killed Walter; he admitted it. He also killed another man, but I don't know his name. It's over, Grim. We've got Walter's killer."

I gave him a feeble smile, and Grim ran the back of his thumb over my cheek. Instead of a hug, I supposed that would have to do.

CHAPTER 26

"The other victim was a man named Edgar Ward," Officer Cowan explained a little while later. "Disappeared six months ago." He scratched his head. "What I can't figure out is how you got Tommy to talk."

"Oh, I have my ways," I replied.

"Those ways almost got you killed, Ms. Provey," Cowan reminded me. "Next time, leave the police work to us. Okay?"

"I will be glad to."

I was sitting in the bed of someone's truck with a blanket wrapped around my shoulders and a Styrofoam cup of hot coffee in my hands. I'd answered every question the police had multiple times. Since my story hadn't changed, I supposed that meant they believed me.

Tommy had admitted to killing Walter. When he came to, all he could mumble was, "Don't let her near me. Please." When he saw me, Tommy screamed. It took four officers to hold him so that he couldn't run off.

It seemed like I might have broken Tommy's brain. If that kept him from killing again, then I was all for it.

"Is there anything that you need from us?" Grim asked Cowan.

Cowan stared down at a clipboard. "No, I think that's about it. But you're not going anywhere, right, Ms. Provey? In case I need to follow up with some questions this week."

"I'm not going anywhere," I said proudly and meant it.

"Let me get you back to your place," Grim said, leading me to his bike.

"How'd you know where I was?" I asked.

His brow furrowed. "It was the strangest thing. I just had a feeling that someone needed help at the ice cream shop. I can't explain it."

I could have explained it, but what was the point? Snow had whispered in Grim's ear. No doubt about that. But I hadn't seen her since she'd disappeared. Where had she gotten off to?

Just as I was climbing onto the back of Grim's bike (we'd get my car in the morning), Snow appeared. "Oh, thank goodness you're okay. I couldn't find anyone to help!"

I frowned and pointed to Grim, whose back was turned.

Snow shook her head. "I didn't see him. I don't know how he got here."

That was strange. If Snow hadn't appeared to Grim, then how had he managed to find me?

Maybe some mysteries were better left unsolved.

The cool night air felt good against my skin as we made our way through town. When we reached the cabin, Grim walked me to the door.

I turned around to say good night, and he said tersely, "I'm coming in. You're not staying alone out here tonight. Not after what you've been through." I lifted my brows, and he replied, "I'll sleep on the couch. I'm a grown man. I know how to keep my hands to myself."

I opened my mouth to protest, but the words didn't come and I didn't want them to. Snow was good company, but in a bind she wasn't exactly the most helpful. After all, she hadn't even found anyone to save me.

Not that I'd needed saving. Because in all actuality, I hadn't. I'd saved myself. Which gave me a great idea.

Grim sat on the couch, and I said, "I'm going to write for a little while. That okay with you?"

"You do whatever it is you need. I can keep myself occupied."

So I wrote. I opened my laptop, and the words spilled out of me. When I looked up at the clock, three hours had passed. It was one in the morning, and Grim was asleep on the couch. I sent Madeleine what I'd written.

She happened to be awake as well, because she immediately responded, *Can't wait to read this. Loved the other pages. I think this is going to be big for you. It'll bring you back from the abyss, Paige.*

I ignored the fact that my agent had said that I was in the abyss as I snapped off lights and went into the bedroom. I planted my face in the bed and fell right to sleep.

When I awoke the next morning, the smell of eggs cooking wafted into the room. I rose and stretched, then found Grim over the stove. Coffee had been made, along with toast, and from somewhere he'd pulled out a jar of strawberry jam.

"Smells heavenly," I said. "Where'd you get the jam?"

He winked over his shoulder. "Went out early this morning and grabbed it. You approve?"

I bit into a corner of the toast. "I very much approve. A man who can cook is never something to frown about."

He smiled. "I wouldn't think so."

He finished cooking and we sat to eat. "Oh my goodness. What did you put into these eggs?" I moaned for added effect. "They're amazing."

"Poultry seasoning."

I arched a brow. "Do you take that with you wherever you go?"

He chuckled, his eyes twinkling. "No. I may have picked that up as well." We ate in silence for a few seconds before he added, "So how do you feel today?"

How did I feel? Amazing. Like I was heading in the right direction for once. I was overcoming what had pinned me down, and I was ready to tackle a new book and my new life.

Well, at least my summer life.

"I feel great."

Grim reached over and placed a hand on mine. "So I was wondering. Would you like to go out tonight?"

Yes! I nearly screamed. But instead I said as demurely as possible, "That would be great."

"And then we can start tracking down the magical book that's still missing."

"Yes," I said.

We finished eating and both of us cleaned up. When everything was washed and put away, I walked Grim to the door.

"Pick you up at seven," he said.

"Perfect."

He brushed his lips over mine, leaving the taste of strawberries on my tongue. When he was gone, I sighed and pressed my back to the wall.

I had a date. A date! With a much younger man. Not that he knew that. Oh my. What would I wear?

I was just about to ransack my closet when a knock came from the door. Was Grim back already?

I opened it, half expecting him to be standing in the doorway with his shirt off. I don't know why his shirt would have been off, but I could hope, couldn't I?

But instead of Grim, a familiar face with heavily made-up eyelids, pink lipstick and dyed black hair stood in front of me.

"Cammie," I gasped. "What are you doing here?"

"Don't look so surprised to see me, Sis. I came to visit you!" She brushed past me, wheeling a suitcase behind her. "Isn't this the cutest little place? Oh, I love it." She dropped her suitcase on the floor and pulled off her straw hat. "Now. Just tell me which bedroom is mine, and I'll make myself right at home."

Oh wow. And just when I thought things were going good. Now it looked like I had family to deal with.

What sort of mayhem will Cammie cause in Paige's life? And how will Paige and Grim's date go?

Find out in POISONED PROSE. Order it now so that you don't miss one minute of fun. Click HERE to order.

If you never want to miss a release, be sure to sign up for my newsletter. You'll have access to sneak peaks of books and will be notified whenever I'm running a sale! Click HERE.

And join my private Facebook Group, the Bless Your Witch club. There, we chat about books and get to know one another. You'll get to do fun things like vote on covers and read unedited chapters. You'll be the first to know insider info. You can join HERE.

ALSO BY AMY BOYLES

SWEET TEA WITCH MYSTERIES

SOUTHERN MAGIC

SOUTHERN SPELLS

SOUTHERN MYTHS

SOUTHERN SORCERY

SOUTHERN CURSES

SOUTHERN KARMA

SOUTHERN MAGIC THANKSGIVING

SOUTHERN MAGIC CHRISTMAS

SOUTHERN POTIONS

SOUTHERN FORTUNES

SOUTHERN HAUNTINGS

SOUTHERN WANDS

SOUTHERN CONJURING

SOUTHERN WISHES

SOUTHERN DREAMS

SOUTHERN MAGIC WEDDING

SOUTHERN OMENS

SOUTHERN JINXED

SOUTHERN BEGINNINGS

SOUTHERN MYSTICS

SOUTHERN CAULDRONS

SOUTHERN HOLIDAY

SOUTHERN ENCHANTED

SOUTHERN TRAPPINGS

SOUTHERN GHOST WRANGLER MYSTERIES

SOUL FOOD SPIRITS

HONEYSUCKLE HAUNTING

THE GHOST WHO ATE GRITS (Crossover with Pepper and Axel from Sweet Tea Witches)

BACKWOODS BANSHEE

MISTLETOE AND SPIRITS

BLESS YOUR WITCH SERIES
SCARED WITCHLESS
KISS MY WITCH
QUEEN WITCH
QUIT YOUR WITCHIN'
FOR WITCH'S SAKE
DON'T GIVE A WITCH
WITCH MY GRITS
FRIED GREEN WITCH
SOUTHERN WITCHING
Y'ALL WITCHES
HOLD YOUR WITCHES

SOUTHERN SINGLE MOM PARANORMAL MYSTERIES
The Witch's Handbook to Hunting Vampires
The Witch's Handbook to Catching Werewolves
The Witch's Handbook to Trapping Demons

ABOUT THE AUTHOR

Hey, I'm Amy,

I write books for folks who crave laugh-out-loud paranormal mysteries. I help bring humor into readers' lives. I've got a Pharm D in pharmacy, a BA in Creative Writing and a Masters in Life.

And when I'm not writing or chasing around two kids (one of which is seven going on seventeen), I can be found antique shopping for a great deal, getting my roots touched up (because that's an every four week job) and figuring out when I can get back to Disney World.

If you're dying to know more about my wacky life, here are three things you don't know about me.

—In college I spent a semester at Marvel Comics working in the X-Men office.

—I worked at Carnegie Hall.

—I grew up in a barbecue restaurant—literally. My parents owned one.

If you want to reach out to me—and I love to hear from readers—you can email me at amyboylesauthor@gmail.com.

Happy reading!

Printed in Great Britain
by Amazon

44813234R10098